**"You're perfect in that bathing suit,"** John said. **"This sort of body made Marilyn Monroe a star."**

Agnes smiled. "I could learn to enjoy your brand of flattery."

"Please don't think I'm flirting." He hesitated. "It *is* flirting, but it's sincere."

She moistened her lips. "I never heard of anyone getting into trouble for kissing on a public beach."

He put a hand on the center of her stomach, caressing the small patch of bare skin the two-piece suit revealed. She trembled under his fingertips.

"We're very secluded back here by the dunes," he agreed. "No one's paying any attention to us."

"I don't feel like Marilyn Monroe, I feel like Doris Day in this suit—and all she ever did was kiss."

The hot breeze drew a strand of red hair across her face. He lifted the hair aside and let the pad of his thumb caress her cheek. "I'm trying to decide which corner of your mouth to kiss first. You have sexy lips, Agnes. I can't tell which lip is nicer. I think it's a tie."

She grinned. "Just kiss me, and I'll help you decide."

When he lowered his mouth to hers, she mewled softly and opened her lips, at first playful as she kissed him, then so intense it was all he could do to keep from snatching her into his arms. A sudden rush of emotion made him feel like a teenager again. . . .

## WHAT ARE *LOVESWEPT* ROMANCES?

They are stories of true romance and touching emotion. We believe those two very important ingredients are constants in our highly sensual and very believable stories in the *LOVESWEPT* line. Our goal is to give you, the reader, stories of consistently high quality that may sometimes make you laugh, sometimes make you cry, but are always fresh and creative and contain many delightful surprises within their pages.

Most romance fans read an enormous number of books. Those they truly love, they keep. Others may be traded with friends and soon forgotten. We hope that each *LOVESWEPT* romance will be a treasure—a "keeper." We will always try to publish

*LOVE STORIES YOU'LL NEVER FORGET*
*BY AUTHORS YOU'LL ALWAYS REMEMBER*

The Editors

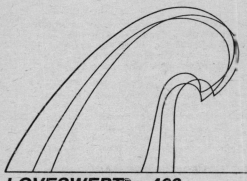

LOVESWEPT® · 468

# Deborah Smith
# Stranger in Camelot

BANTAM BOOKS
NEW YORK · TORONTO · LONDON · SYDNEY · AUCKLAND

STRANGER IN CAMELOT

*A Bantam Book / May 1991*

ISBN 0-553-44111-6

*For Ann White and our phone bills*

# One

*This is the last farewell, my lady, my love.*

The tender words of a doomed English knight reached across more than eight hundred years and once again filled Aggie Hamilton's eyes with tears. Dismayed, she brushed a calloused fingertip across her damp cheeks. Her reaction was beginning to worry her.

The powerful story of Sir Miles of Norcross, and his love for his wife, Eleanor, had taken over Aggie's imagination for the past month. But Sir Miles's diary and prayer book were worth a small fortune, and she couldn't afford to let her infatuation with him get out of control.

She jumped as another round of thunder bowled across the black sky. Beyond her bedroom window the sultry Florida night was filling with heat and electricity, and the wind rushed through her white curtains like boiling ocean surf. She could imagine the white breakers flinging themselves against the beaches in St. Augustine, ten miles away.

Her emotions were in the same fever.

Her hands quivering, she placed the notebook pages covered with her grandfather's neat, scholarly translation back into the metal security box along with its more precious contents, Sir Miles's original diary and his prayer book. She'd never suspected that her grandfather was capable of harboring such an unnervingly valuable possession. Or of bequeathing it to her. Every time she thought of how much the books must be worth, her mouth went dry.

Because she didn't want to sell them.

When lightning flashed outside her window Aggie jumped. She turned up the volume on the small radio beside her bed to catch more details from the announcer of tornado warnings for St. Augustine and the surrounding areas.

A chill ran up her back. She had to check on her mares. Sliding out of bed, she shoved the tail of her short nightgown into cut-off jeans then laced hiking boots on her bare feet. She carried the security box to the room next to hers and dropped it into a bottom file drawer of a scarred old desk. She locked the drawer hurriedly, using its tarnished key, and tossed the key into a flower vase filled with silk begonias.

No time, no time. The thunder seemed to rumble the message to her, and she wondered why she wasted precious time on daydreams.

She ran to her front porch. A half dozen ugly, fat, adoring dogs huddled around her legs as she stared anxiously into the storm.

Trouble was brewing in the night.

Aggie grabbed a flashlight from a porch shelf. As she crossed the sandy yard past the outbuildings, large raindrops slapped her face. Behind the main barn the pine trees swayed wildly. She climbed a pasture gate and stumbled when her boots sank into the churned sand on the other side.

She cupped her hands around her mouth and yelled into the tempest. *"Val-en-tine!"* Squinting, she saw her six mares galloping toward her from the pasture's far side. One ran slightly ahead of them. Valentine, undoubtedly. She was always the leader.

*With a rider on her back.*

Astonished, Aggie shook her head to clear the phantom from it. Her imagination had been overloaded lately. The darkness absorbed the mares again. Aggie's heart pounded. She whistled and called toward the racing shadows. "Val-en-tine! Come here, Val-en-tine!"

When a burst of lightning whitened the darkness, Aggie was already running down the pasture's edge along the pine forest, drenched and shaking with fear. Moving from tree to tree in the pouring rain, she gritted her teeth when the wind threw a small limb against her side.

It tangled in her nightgown, and when she jerked it loose it tore a long gash in the cotton material. She tried distractedly to cover her exposed breast, then gave up.

The limber pine trees bent like flowers in a stiff breeze. At the edge of the pasture the flat Florida landscape stretched into infinity across a universe of tall grass. Aggie peered helplessly into the blackness as streamers of her long hair plastered themselves over her eyes.

She tripped on a clump of sharp palmetto grass and fell to her hands and knees, while the flashlight tumbled into the grass, turning off as it rolled. Her dogs hovered nearby, whimpering in the cover of the pines.

Aggie's raspy breaths were lost in the slashing rain and wind. The thunder crashed around her as she slung her hair back and staggered to her feet.

The night snapped open as lightning flared. Aggie gasped, both hands raised defensively, her fingers knotting in her torn gown. *Yes, someone was riding Valentine.*

The phantom was tall. A cape flared around him in the tearing wind. He was riding straight out of the night toward her. Sir Miles would have been this dramatic,

Aggie thought, riding out of the darkness. Then she shook her head furiously. She was losing her mind over a medieval fantasy.

Within the space of a few frantic heartbeats the man and the horses closed in on her. Aggie broke her stunned stillness and waved her arms to halt them. She wouldn't let herself be run over by a phantom or trampled by her own imagination. She was too practical for that.

"Val-en-tiiine! Whooa!"

The other mares fanned out and kept running when they saw her, but Valentine began to slow, as if controlled by the apparition astride her back. Lightning illuminated his outstretched arm as the mare loped the last few paces toward Aggie. Her blood thundered like the storm. *He was reaching toward her.*

Then her ears filled with the moan of wood being ripped apart behind her. Aggie pivoted blindly in the darkness and rain, staring at a pine that had broken in the middle. The top lurched crazily.

The mares brushed past her on either side, snorting, flinging soggy clumps of sand with their hooves. Valentine slid to a stop and bumped her in the back. Aggie lost her balance and nearly fell as Valentine twisted sideways, prancing.

The horseman reached down and grabbed Aggie's shoulder.

Terrified, she whirled toward him. What was happening to her simple life? She'd been waiting for something or someone to break the spell that had captured her. To break it, or make it real.

"What are you doing here?" she screamed up at the phantom, twisting out of his grasp as she did. The wind howled around them as if filled with spirits. "What do you want?"

She heard the whoosh of a torn tree branch a second before it struck her head. Then there was just the darkness and the phantom, who absorbed her last conscious thought when he called her name. It seemed he had answered her question.

The publicity photographs hadn't come close to doing her justice, John Bartholomew decided as he hurriedly carried the woman into her house. Of course, the photos had been taken more than twelve years before, when she left show business.

She wasn't the girl-next-door teenager anymore. Good. He'd been struggling to picture the mature Aggie Hamilton, and he hadn't wanted to see her as that cute, oddly vulnerable-looking kid. There was too much at stake for him to risk feeling sentimental toward her.

No problem there, he grumbled to himself. The half-conscious woman he carried into the small, weathered house and placed on the old couch was disarmingly voluptuous compared to the skinny teenager, and the hair that had been done in tomboy braids was a thick, curly mane, even when wet.

And photos hadn't hinted at her intriguing scent—a mixture of hay, spices, rainwater. In his arms she felt achingly soft but not delicate. Her ruddy fists—even when knocked nearly senseless she never unclenched them—impressed him with their determination.

*Americans grow their thieves lovely but tough,* he thought.

Scowling, John tucked a throw pillow under her head. Then he strode into her kitchen and ran water over a dish towel. He'd seen too many knocked heads and been knocked in the head too often himself to be very alarmed about her condition. Still, his heart was tripping along a bit too fast for its unfeeling self, he thought wryly. Had to be the storm's effect. And seeing her in all the thunder and lightning, braced against the elements, fighting them. And seeing her get hurt. All of it had given him the feeling that she'd been waiting for him. It made him feel guilty. What rubbish!

John ran back to the living room and bent over her, his yellow poncho streaming water onto the pale, glistening skin of her face and neck. He removed the poncho and tossed it aside then cupped her head in one hand, while he wiped the cloth over the scraped place at the top of her forehead. A nasty bruise was swelling there.

She continued to move her head weakly, frowning and squinting. John smoothed back her sopping red hair. With what he hoped was cynicism he studied her face. Still a girlish package, with those apple-round cheeks and that tipped nose, he decided. But the sexy mouth gave her away. Her mouth had grown up a long time ago, according to the stories about her. He reminded himself that her past wasn't as pretty as she was.

Finally he looked at her breasts. The soaked gown didn't leave any secrets about their size, shape, or general magnificence, and the torn place neatly framed one breast and its rosy, upthrust nipple. A drop of rainwater perched there. Her restless movements made it slide onto her blue-veined skin and disappear beneath the gown's ragged edge.

John was dismayed but not surprised when blood rushed to his belly and tightened him. He never hesitated to admire a woman, the fewer clothes on her, the better. But he didn't want to admire a hurt, helpless one who had no choice in the matter.

He had nothing else to cover her with, so he removed his soggy white pullover and draped it along her torso. The pullover hid her from neck to thighs. John shook his head at her long, sculpted legs. He'd covered what he could. He deserved to enjoy looking at the rest.

He knelt beside the couch and pressed the dishcloth to her head again. The rainwater inside his khaki trousers made him itch to strip his clothes off. With grim humor he wondered how quickly the sight of a tall, hairy man wearing nothing but briefs would shock the lady back to her senses.

The other women who had seen him that way over the years had not been shocked, of course, but, well, delightfully astonished. But Aggie Hamilton would probably punch him with those hard little fists and call the local constable.

"Agnes?" he said gently, pressing the cloth to her forehead. "Miss Hamilton?"

Her hands finally unfurled and moved limply toward her head. She touched her face with tentative fingertips, bumped his hands, stopped, then sighed. Even with her eyes still closed her expression seemed confused—or was it hopeful? "Sir Miles," she murmured.

John was so startled at hearing his ancestor's name that he drew back abruptly, forgetting gentleness. After studying her for a moment, grim determination took over. She had the books. This proved it.

Blinking rapidly, she opened her eyes and stared into space, wincing with pain. Slowly her gaze shifted to him. He watched her eyes focus then widen with alarm.

"You're all right," he assured her distractedly, squeezing her hand for a moment. "You were hit on the head by a tree branch. I carried you to your house. Please don't be afraid of me."

"Who are you and what were you doing in my pasture?"

He started to tell her the truth. He'd come here planning to tell her, to confront her. But he couldn't start making trouble while she was hurt and groggy. The way she'd said "Sir Miles" made a shiver run up his spine. She'd caressed the name as if it meant something special to her.

"Who are you?" she repeated. "Quit givin' me that stare and say something."

"Miss Hamilton, relax. First things first. Are you all right?"

She gingerly touched the knot on her forehead. Her gaze bored into him, not sidetracked by the pain. "I said, Who are you?"

He planned quickly and came up with an evasive answer. "I'm a tourist. I was looking for your campground when my Jeep broke down. I climbed over a fence along the road—your fence, apparently—and started walking. I hoped to find the campsite or your house."

"What were you doing with my horses?"

"Nothing wicked, I assure you." He chuckled, trying very hard to distract himself from the intriguing mixture of colors in her eyes. The irises were gray toward the center, darkening outward to soft blue, and rimmed in dark blue at the perimeters. He could understand how a camera would fall in love with those eyes.

He leaned forward again and stroked the wet cloth over her bruise. An injured woman could turn a man to mush. All his protective instincts rose to the surface. And it was pleasing to touch her, more pleasing than touching any other woman he could recall. Glancing down at her generous breasts making hills under his shirt, he admitted that his plan might become much more personal than he'd expected.

*You're no gentleman, Bartholomew.*

"I'm terribly lazy," he told her. "I saw the horses and decided that searching for your campground would be a great deal more pleasant if I had four hooves under me."

"That mare you were galloping is in foal."

"Eight hooves, then." He laughed, saw her stern expression soften a little, and knew that his charm was working. "I could see that she was pregnant. I didn't encourage her to take off like a rocket. But she didn't ask for my permission. With nothing but my belt snugged around her nose as a rein, she didn't have to."

"You're English, aren't you?"

"Yes. From London."

The information upset her. He could see her withdrawing, wariness and surprise cloaking her eyes. Dull anger grew inside him. She had the books. That was why meeting an Englishman startled her. If she was this nervous about her secret, he'd have a fight when she learned why he'd come to find her.

But maybe she didn't need to know. Maybe he could coax her into telling him about the books, if he played his cards right. "Is there a problem?" John asked.

"No. Nothing. I don't get many foreign tourists, that's all. By the way, the campground is on the other side of the woods, not here. This is my home. My ranch."

"All right. Now that we've got the introduction settled, let's take care of you. How do you feel?"

"Fine." She pushed upright and wedged herself into a corner of the couch, inching farther away from him. He noticed his pullover was about to fall down, but couldn't decide how to point that out to her delicately.

"I fear you're being brave. We should give a name to that small mountain growing on your forehead. Honor it, as if it were a monument. I believe we could charge admission. Perhaps turn you into a state park. Mount Agnes State Park. Yes, I rather like that."

His teasing earned a vague smile from her, though suspicion still clouded her eyes. "This is like listening to Richard Burton try to do stand-up comedy. Or being heckled by a British Don Rickles."

"I'm sorry," he said quickly. "I wasn't trying to annoy you. Only make you smile. How do you feel, really?"

"Like a cartoon character who's been hit with a hammer. I'm sure there are stars and little birds circling my head."

"No stars, not in this weather." Steady rain drummed on the house, rattling the porch's tin roof. Cool, sweet air had filled the night, carrying with it a hint of salt marshes. Thunder growled faintly in the distance. John had trouble paying attention.

"Did you notice where my horses went?" she asked, straightening.

"Sssh. They're safely gathered in the woods. The worst of the storm is over."

"I have to go check on them."

He pretended to study the floor lamp behind the couch. "You'll need dry clothes, first."

She looked down at herself. "Oh, boy." She calmly lifted his pullover shirt and held it over her chest. But her cheeks were red. "Thanks for the loan."

"Sorry about the embarrassment."

"Don't apologize for being gallant." She looked at him with an intrigued expression, then glanced at the faded chintz-covered couch. The cushions where she'd lain had a wet outline of her body. Frowning, she wiped drops of water from a torn place in the upholstery. "Guess it's a good thing I donated the priceless antiques to the Smithsonian."

"Yes, I like this style much better."

"I must get up. See about the mares."

John placed a hand on her shoulder when she started to scoot past him. "That's a nasty bump, Miss Hamilton. Your horses are fine. Rest."

She stared at him, then at his broad, darkly haired hand. Her breasts rose and fell swiftly under his shirt. Her eyes darted anxiously to his bare chest, then back to his face. She gave him a cold look of warning.

John casually dropped his hand to his knee. She was looking at him the way a woman did when she distrusted men—all men—intensely. He felt even more protective toward her. "You don't have to be nervous. I know this is an odd situation, but you've got nothing to worry about where I'm concerned."

That might be untrue in some ways, he thought a bit guiltily.

She shuddered and exhaled a long, tired breath. "Sorry. Don't take it personally." Tilting her head, she studied him with fascination again. "I guess you're the first man who rescued me from anything, and I keep wanting to pinch myself to see if I'm dreaming."

"Please, no pinching. You've got one bruise already." He was glad to see her smile at his teasing. "I'll check on your horses for you, if you like. All right, Agnes?"

"Who told you my name?" He sat back on his heels to give her space. He knew he was too large and brawny to look harmless, but a lot of women found that appealing. He hoped Agnes Hamilton was one of them.

"You're listed on the bulletin board at the crossroads grocery," he said. "'Hamilton Lake and Campground. Aggie Hamilton, owner.' Your advertisement is right under the one for a fishing supplies store. I was looking at 'Live Worms and Shrimp—Cheap,' and then I found you."

She smiled again. "There are other campgrounds listed on that board."

"True. I'm lucky, I suppose." He held out the wet dishcloth as if it were a gift. She took it slowly and dabbed it against her bruise. Her hair was a mass of wet ringlets that twirled several inches below her shoulders.

She could have stepped from a shower. Easy enough to envision her naked and surrounded by steam, John thought. Too easy. "I was trying to lead the horses safely into the woods," he told her. "Not using one for a free ride."

With painful effort she cocked a dark-red brow and studied him solemnly. "What's a British tourist doing so far off the beaten track? You ought to fire your travel agent."

"I wanted to roam the back roads of America. I'm here for a whole month. I decided to rent a Jeep and go wherever the mood took me. Besides, this isn't so secluded. I hear that St. Augustine is a lovely, large town. And it's close by, isn't it?"

"Fifteen minutes." She held her head and shut her eyes. Her pale complexion, sprinkled with almond-colored freckles across the nose, was turning a sallow color. She had exactly five freckles. John had counted them. "I'm a little dizzy," she said.

He rose to his feet quickly. "I think an X ray of that lovely noggin is in order. If you'll trust me to drive your car, and you'll give me highway directions, I'll carry you to hospital."

"Carry me to hospital?" she mimicked gently, doing a surprisingly good imitation of his accent. "I don't like hospitals, but the way you put it, going to one sounds pretty quaint."

"'Kindness it is that brings forth kindness always.'"

"Hmmm, a philosophy lesson."

"The ancient Greeks had a way with words. 'One who knows how to show and to accept kindness will be a friend better than any possession.' Sophocles. About four hundred B.C."

The look on Aggie Hamilton's face said that she had doubts about a man who tried to impress her by quoting Sophocles. Getting off the couch with slow, careful movements, she recited darkly, "'Skipper, I smell something fishy around here.'" She cut her eyes at him. "Gilligan. About 1967."

He bit back a rich laugh and latched a hand under her arm as she stood up. "Thanks for your help," she said abruptly. She held the dishcloth to her head and peered up at him from under an orange chicken embroidered on the material. "This is a strange night. A strange night." She seemed to be mulling those words, lost in some private bewilderment. "But I appreciate what you did for my horses. And thanks for bringing me inside. And for offering to drive—"

"I'll blush if you don't stop."

"You don't look like a blusher to me."

"You're wrong, dear lady. Right now, you're making me feel very shy."

She stared at him open-mouthed. John had been joking, and he was intrigued when she looked as if she believed him.

"Whatever or whoever you are, you're unique," she said finally, and there was an awed tone in her voice. "And I'm very glad to meet you."

John caught his breath and stared back at her. She was a good deal shorter than he, but not a short woman. He happened to be taller than average. She was average, he'd say. At least in height.

The sweet womanly smell of her, the voluptuous body, and the sincerity in her upturned face had an extraordinary pull on him. She was a solid fifteen on a scale of one to ten. Never average. Never.

"Come along," John urged. "We'll talk more on the way to hospital."

"You *still* haven't told me your name."

"True. I apologize. Here." He pulled a damp but expensive-looking leather wallet from a trouser pocket. "My passport, my international driving permit, and my credit cards. Look. I even have a card for the London library. No scoundrel would dare own such a respectable thing."

She peered at the open wallet as he turned the plastic leaves containing his I.D. She squinted and swayed in place. John wanted to put an arm around her, but he knew better than to try, at the moment. "Thirty-seven years old, tall, dark, and able to read," she recited vaguely. "And your name is . . ."

"John. John Bartholomew." Very carefully, watching her closely, he added, "Just a modern-day knight in shining khaki, at your service, my lady."

She looked up at him with a stunned expression on

her face. The last remnant of color fled from her cheeks. "Why did you say that?"

"You seem to have an interest in knights. When you were semi-conscious, you called me 'Sir Miles.'"

When she fainted, John caught her in his arms. He felt guilty but victorious.

She was more confused than sick, more worried than in pain. Aggie stared up at the emergency room's white ceiling, lost in frantic thought. Her back was stiff with tension, barely touching the gurney's white-sheeted mattress beneath her. Each time a doctor or nurse walked past the white curtain that walled off her cubicle, she flinched.

She wanted John Bartholomew to stay out in the waiting room. She wanted him to fade back into the night. Into the centuries past?

The instant she'd looked up into those intense hazel eyes she'd felt his power, his easy command of a woman's attention. Some chord of excitement vibrated inside her because of his elegantly wicked face, with its wreath of dark, coarse hair slicked around it in wet tendrils. The picture of worldly charm had a trace of dark brown beard stubble. But there had been sincere gentleness in his expression, and nothing but kindness in his hands.

The phantom had human form, and that form was mesmerizing.

Aggie groaned with disgust. Sir Miles of Norcross had *not* come to life to haunt her. Or was it to seduce her? Or to find out why his diary and prayer book had never been returned to his native England?

She sank her fingers into the hair on the unbruised side of her head and tugged in self-rebuke. She had to stop thinking this way.

John's pullover, which she now wore, carried a trace of his cologne, and every time she inhaled she felt as if he still had his arms around her. Her damp shorts were clammy on her stomach, and her sockless feet felt cold. But that wasn't why she shivered.

John's question had been harmless, she repeated doggedly. No one knew about her books. *She* hadn't even known about them until two months ago, when she'd opened the bank deposit box left to her in her grandfather's will.

"Agnes? May I come in?"

She turned her head sharply toward John's deep, melodic voice. He looked at her politely from one corner of the cubicle where he'd pulled the curtains aside and draped them dramatically over his shoulder.

Aggie caught her breath. The director of the St. Augustine Theatrical Society would kill to have this man and his dulcet voice in the summer production of *Macbeth*. John Bartholomew as Macbeth. Hmmm. No, Hamlet. A lusty-looking Hamlet with shoulders wide enough to carry Denmark.

"Agnes?" he said again, studying her closely.

"It's Aggie."

"Do you mind if I call you Agnes? It's such a lovely name."

"Call me Agnes if you want to, but nobody else does."

"Good. I love being different. Bloody arrogant English pride, you know." He smiled widely. "Fair Agnes, may I enter?"

But he was already halfway inside the cubicle. She wondered which dominated—the polite John or the John who had taken action first then asked permission. "You're in," she replied.

He let the curtains fall behind him and stepped close to the gurney. He looked rugged and indelicate against the curtain's pristine background. Someone had given him a wrinkled white orderly's top to wear. Its elbow-length sleeves displayed muscular forearms where sinews and veins struggled artfully under the bondage of skin and hair. His khaki trousers had dried stiff and tight to his straight hips and long legs. Might as well be looking at the bottom half of a nude statue after it had been covered in papier-mâché, Aggie thought. She reluctantly dragged her gaze up to his face.

He smiled at her. His smile was so kind it only heightened the primitive, sensual thrust of his lips. Then he sat down on the side of the gurney, drawing one knee up. "The doctor tells me your head's not cracked a bit. She suspects your fainting was brought on by a combination of the injury plus physical exhaustion. She said something about you working three jobs. She seems to know a great deal about you."

"We're acquainted. I sold her a quarter-horse colt last spring."

"Do you really work three jobs?"

"Yeah. I write a few articles for one of the local newspapers, and four nights a week I tend bar at one of the tourist pubs over in St. Augustine. No big deal."

"Why so many jobs?"

"Need the green stuff. Moolah. Bucks. Dough. Cold hard cash."

"You Americans have the most inventive words for simple things. I like your imagination."

"I like to imagine that I have some. Money, that is. I operate my quarter-horse business on a *very* slender budget. In fact, I'd say that it's so slender, it's anorexic."

"Don't you have any help?"

"Nope."

A little subdued, Aggie pushed herself upright, trying desperately to ignore the pressure of John Bartholomew's long, muscular thigh against her hip. He smelled of rain, horsehair, and a smoky masculine scent that made her think about kissing his neck.

"Remind me to have my head examined regularly," she muttered under her breath.

"I beg your pardon? I didn't catch that."

"Never mind. I mutter to myself in public. It's a job hazard of the one-woman ranching business. I spend a lot of time talking to horses."

"Would you feel more comfortable if I neighed and pawed the ground?"

"Maybe." She stuck a hand into a back pocket of her jeans and scraped out a crumbling, half-melted lump of sugar. She thrust it toward him on her palm. "Have a treat, stud."

She was only joking but he smiled, bent forward, and took the sugar with a single deep, sucking motion of his lips. His tongue touched her palm as he finished. He swallowed, smiling at her mischievously the whole time. "Hmmm. Sweet. And the sugar was good too."

Aggie slowly dropped her hand into her lap. Her palm tingled. The damp, coarse texture of his tongue was now imprinted on her memory.

They looked at each other, she feeling awkard, he appearing calm. "Be still a moment," he ordered mildly. He brushed something from her temple, his fingertip warm and gentle. "A drop of antiseptic was creeping down. "He touched the scraped skin over the knot on her forehead. Aggie inhaled softly. His touch was so careful; it didn't hurt a bit.

"What kind of work do you do, back in London?" she asked. "Give massages to butterflies?"

He smiled. "I own a chain of hobby stores. In other words, I sell model kits—airplanes, ships, cars, that sort of thing."

Impossible, Aggie thought. She couldn't picture this man in such a tame setting. Selling toys to grown-ups or slaving over bits of balsa wood and cheap chrome? Impossible. She couldn't picture him as a business manager, wearing a suit and shuffling papers with those big paws of his.

"You've always been in the hobby-store business?" she asked, watching him closely.

He nodded. "I inherited the business from my father. In fact, I'm the third generation of Bartholomews to run it."

She decided she liked the contrast between his profession and his macho appearance. Actually, he'd done nothing to make her think he was less than civilized. It was only that she knew the opposite kind of man so well, and she couldn't shrug off a feeling that there was danger beneath John Bartholomew's confident hazel eyes. Aggie sighed. Maybe she'd been lonely and cynical for too long.

"As soon as the nurse brings my paperwork, we can hit the road."

"If you don't mind, I'll go to my Jeep when we return and gather my camping gear. Do you feel well enough to drive home after you leave me at your campground?"

"Sure. It's only a couple of minutes on a dirt road through the woods." Guilt caught in her throat. Aggie frowned at him while she considered her next words. "Ummm, John, after all you've done for me, I can't dump you out in the dark and rain to set up your tent. You're welcome to stay in my barn tonight."

"Agnes, you're a love."

"I have six fat but protective dogs." She met his eyes with an amused, slightly warning gaze. "And a shotgun that could turn you into Swiss cheese."

"I rest convinced, dear lady. Now please be convinced in return. I'm a very trustworthy tourist, who'll cause you no grief. I'm happy to have rescued you earlier this evening, and I won't make you regret it."

She gazed at him in growing wonder. Gentle, noble, and gallant. The same as Sir Miles of Norcross, the knight who had captured her imagination. But John

Bartholomew was no warrior, just a businessman from London on vacation.

Simple. Then why was her heart pounding?

The May night was so misty that every breath of air was damp and warm. The mares stood in a line along the wooden fence, the mist swirling each time they breathed into it.

Aggie thought them beautiful, as usual, but the moody atmosphere played on her unsettled emotions. She was weak with fatigue; her head hurt, and her senses were alert to the man beside her.

"All safe and well," he said, stroking a hand down one mare's neck. "And all pregnant, from the looks of their stomachs."

"Yeah, I'm running an equine maternity ward. You're looking at a hundred thousand dollars in horse futures, just waiting to be born this summer."

He nodded toward the whitewashed wooden barn that backed up to the fence. "I hate to take their bedrooms."

"I only bring them in at feeding time. If you sleep past eight, you'll be sharing breakfast in bed with them."

"As long as they don't slurp their tea, I won't complain."

Aggie wearily motioned for him to follow her. Her dogs gamboled around his feet, licking his pants legs. They were certainly impressing him with their fierceness, she noticed.

Hoisting a backpack to one shoulder and his sleeping bag to the other, he kept pace with her easily. She sensed his gaze on her as she stepped into the barn and flicked a light switch. A line of bare bulbs glowed down the center of the ten-stall building. The floor was covered in fresh sawdust. The wooden stalls and their doors, though scarred from being kicked, chewed, and rubbed over the years, were solid and respectable.

"Nothing fancy, but it's home," she told him. "Pick any clean stall you like. Or a less-clean one, if you want to dream about organic gardening."

"I'll be fine." He set his gear down and turned toward her, frowning. "But will you be? No more fainting, fair Agnes."

"Nope. I'm going to get a good night's sleep. Tomorrow you'll meet the real Aggie Hamilton. Fresh. Spunky."

"Methinks the lady will be even more intriguing."

Chuckling darkly, she went to the big open doors and took a deep breath of night air before she turned to say good night. It didn't help. Under the dim lights he looked shadowy and compelling, a mystery waiting to draw her in. She was even more afraid of him.

"Do you always talk that way?" she asked sharply. "'Methinks.' 'Lady this and lady that.' Like Robin Hood in a singles bar?"

"No, sometimes I don't talk at all. When a woman is tense, the right sort of action is far more effective."

He walked over to her before she realized what he intended and kissed her on the cheek. He didn't startle her like a thief; his kiss was a lingering, mobile caress. He sampled her skin like a gourmet tasting a sherbet.

Aggie wanted to be angry. Instead she stood there gazing up at him in a daze. He laughed. "You bring out the gallant in me. I'm helpless."

"I'm still trying to decide if you're for real."

"Oh, yes." He bowed to her slightly. "Forgive me for being so coy. I'm a dedicated medieval history buff, you see, and I tend to forget that I sound pretentious at times. I've been accused of living in the past. Very far in the past, in fact."

Aggie came back to earth with a jolt. "Is that why you asked me about the name I said when I was groggy?"

"Yes. Is this 'Sir Miles' someone you've been studying? Are you interested in medieval history?"

"A little." Caution made knots in her stomach. "I must have read about somebody with that name."

"We have a lot in common. We both love horses, and we're both caught up in the past. I look forward to staying at your campground and visiting with you."

Aggie nodded woodenly. She didn't want him to stay at her campground. Or in the neighborhood. Or in the country. And especially not in her thoughts.

"Good night, Lady Agnes," he said, smiling as he bowed to her.

Aggie nodded vaguely and walked away, feeling worried and defensive. But underneath, a traitorous little part of herself whispered, *Good night, Sir John.*

# *Two*

John woke up with an ugly taste in his mouth. He hadn't come here to manipulate and deceive anyone, but to get what was his. He knew how it felt to be the victim of lies. An enemy's lies had cost him his career with Scotland Yard. Lies had put him in prison. Now, using lies to charm Agnes Hamilton disgusted him.

His problem wasn't with her, but with her grandfather. Sam Hamilton, an officer in the American army who had befriended John's grandparents during the war. They had lost almost everything in the heavy bombing of the countryside and had trusted Sam to help them protect two family heirlooms—the irreplaceable medieval books of their most famous ancestor, Sir Miles of Norcross. A powerful knight in the early years of King Henry II's reign, Sir Miles had been unjustly accused of treason, imprisoned in the Tower of London, and eventually executed there. In history books he was described as a man the peasantry regarded as fair and kind. His wife Eleanor, too. A faithful servant of his king, he'd been the innocent victim of political intrigues.

The diary Sir Miles had written for Eleanor while imprisoned in the Tower was a testament to their love and dignity. His legend was based on it.

And then that damned American army officer, Sam Hamilton, had stolen it, and also Sir Miles's prayer book. John's mother had been too young to know the officer's name. Later in the war, her parents died, so the officer's identity was lost forever. John's mother had grown up in orphanages and foster homes.

Even now John grimaced as he recalled her stories of poverty and abuse. She and his father, the son of another ruined family of old lineage, had both been orphaned and neglected after the war. When they married they shared their emotional scars, but they never overcame them.

John clenched his hands. How different their lives might have been if they'd had those books to sell! How different *his* boyhood would have been if they'd been able to care for themselves, and him, better.

Kicking himself for brooding over family history, John sat up on his sleeping bag and looked around Agnes's barn, fiercely rubbing his hands over his face and bare chest to wake himself. Drawing his knees up, he leaned his arms on them while he thought about her. He liked calling her Agnes instead of Aggie. She was a tough little bird with a smart mouth, but classy.

There was more to her than the pride she wore like diamonds. The scandals in her past must have taught her to look at the world with that scrappy I'm-better-than-you-think-I-am attitude. John recognized her feelings, because he felt the same way.

His body reacted with bawdy excitement to his thoughts about her. He glanced down at the only item of clothing he could bear to sleep in during the muggy Florida nights. The blue and white striped swim trunks weren't baggy enough for his feelings this morning. Agnes Hamilton filled him inside with too much annoyance, admiration, and pure blinding lust.

He was definitely no gentleman, not the way the English upper-class defined it, even though his blood was as blue as the Queen's. Bloodlines didn't mean anything without money, because money bought respectability and his family had lost both.

John rose quickly and went in search of a water hose and a cold dousing. Agnes had the books that were rightfully his by his mother's inheritance, and if he could coax her, and them, into his hands, he'd be rich, and gentlemen be damned.

Aggie lay among the jumbled white sheets of her bed and trembled, her emotions ragged and her skin so warm that she threw the sheets back and fanned herself with the tail of her floppy white T-shirt.

She might as well have turned on every fan in the house and surrounded herself with them. The heat was internal, and thinking about John Bartholomew brought it to the surface.

Aggie glanced at the digital clock on her nightstand and saw that the time was only a little past seven. Good. He might still be asleep. She hoped to take a peek at him before he woke up. Strengthen her resolve. See if he snored, like a mortal human.

She got out of bed and, holding a hand against her head, groaned. She felt better than last night, but the pain still jiggled in her skull. She had the feeling that if someone shook her, her eyes would bounce like the beads in the plastic eyes of the stuffed baby alligator on her dresser.

She didn't approve of stuffing alligators, but Grandpa had given her the thing as a welcoming gift when she'd moved in five years ago. For that reason, she treasured it.

She'd named it Al, for Al Sheffield, the tough little Hollywood agent who had put an end to what was left of her career, at her request. Because Al had been good at breaking contracts, she'd been able to move here before the last of her pride was gone. Every year she sent Al a birthday card and in his honor kissed his stuffed reptilian namesake on its scaly nose.

She took off her T-shirt so that she could strap her generous breasts into an industrial-strength sports bra. She jerked the T-shirt back into place and glowered at her chest. Let John Bartholomew have fun staring at this shield of cotton-polyester.

Brushing past Al to the collection of bandannas hanging from her dresser mirror, she chose a faded blue one then pulled her tangled black hair back with it. Next she belted baggy khaki work shorts over torn white panties that the dogs had stolen from the laundry and used for a tug-of-war. The panties were comfortable and they still did their duty. That was all that mattered. Finally she stuck her feet into tall white crew socks and ankle-high hiking boots, with bright orange laces that she wound around the tops.

Clumping outside to the porch, she opened the big metal trash can where she stored dry dog food and scooped the chow into the dogs' communal pan, spilling food on the warped wooden floor as she did. Her attention was on the barn a hundred yards away. The open doors, twice her height and swathed in delicate jasmine vines, resembled the entrance to a dark cave. Now it had a bear inside.

She wiped damp palms on her shorts. Drawing a deep breath of dewy, sunshine-filled air, she marched to the barn. Inside, sunlight filtered through cracks in the boards, and the only sound was the resident mouse scratching around in its cranny along the feedroom wall.

In the last stall she found his sleeping bag and backpack. So he hadn't faded into the night's mist without a trace.

She stopped in the center of the hallway, listening with taut nerves and looking toward the other set of double doors that led to the corral and pasture. One door stood open. She cocked her head and heard the low hum of the barn's water pipe as it strained to full throttle.

Aggie jumped when a loud growl of masculine discomfort sounded outside, followed by the splashing of water. She hurried into the corral, the soft sand sucking at her shoes as if reluctant to let her see what was around the corner of the barn.

Aggie sprang to the wooden fence where it butted against the building then craned her head around.

He might as well have been naked, considering how the swim trunks were plastered to him and how low they'd settled on his lean hips. He had his eyes shut and his head tilted back to catch the full force of the water hose he held above him. Water drenched him, splattered off the chiseled nose and roughly planed cheekbones, and ran in frothy torrents down a broad chest covered in dark hair.

When the streams reached his stomach they snaked along smooth, honey-colored skin with a converging trail of dark hair at the center. At the top of his trunks the hair spread out again and hinted at the different coarseness farther down. Not very far, considering how little of his belly was left to the imagination. It was obvious that his trunks were held up only by the part of him that refused to remain flat, even when doused with cold water. The water was innocent, but the way it caressed him was a lesson in intimacy.

Aggie clenched the top of the fence and studied him raptly, telling herself she was only responding to what Madison Avenue advertising companies had discovered long ago, that water streaming down a handsome male body was one of the most provocative sights in the world. Millions of women had bought extra soap because of commercials based on this.

Well, not *quite* like this, because commercials were never X-rated.

Aggie couldn't help noticing that his trunks trapped water and allowed only the most tempting little streams to escape. They sought paths through the smooth, dark hair on his long legs. She stared at a trickle that slid slowly down the heavy muscle atop one of his thighs. Those water molecules had certainly had an interesting trip.

Buying soap was the last thing on her mind.

Feeling bad for watching him in secret, she started to climb down and leave, but he opened his eyes and caught sight of her. Aggie halted, one foot on the middle fence board, the other about to settle on the board below it. The thick sole of her hiking boot slipped on the board's painted edge, still damp from the night's rain. Aggie's foot and leg plunged between the boards, and she cursed. A second later she was straddling the fence halfway up and flailing about with her arms for a grip.

Lady Agnes, indeed!

As she struggled to pull her leg back, and her rump began to slide toward the ground, she was grimly aware of John Bartholomew tossing the hose aside and coming to help her. He scaled the tall fence so fast that he made a smooth vault from the middle board and then over, landing right beside her. His large, bare feet sprayed her with fine particles of sand.

"Let me, Agnes," he said kindly, without a trace of amusement. Then he put his hands under her arms and pulled her upward. She felt like an ant being lifted by a crane.

"When I was a kid I took ten years of dance classes. For all that damned trouble I shouldn't have ended up with the grace of an armadillo."

"Even a swan has awkward moments." Her feet dangled off the ground. He lifted her higher and kissed the tip of her nose. She thought her breasts were being stroked by every hair and muscle of his chest as he set her down. When she took a shaky step back, he cupped his hands on her shoulders to steady her. "Good morning," he said pleasantly.

"Mornin'."

She busily adjusted her bandanna and smoothed her shorts, trying to ignore her jumbled emotions and his glistening body. "I didn't mean to interrupt your shower."

"Thank goodness you did. I was in agony. Didn't your advertisement say there are shower stalls with hot water at your campground? I hope so. My nobility would get icicles on it if I had to take a cold shower every morning."

"Look, John, that's something we've got to talk about." Aggie stepped back again, forcing him to drop his hands from her shoulders.

"My icicles?" He eyed her hopefully, smiling.

She suddenly felt like a jerk. "I was too addled last night to remember my rules. The campground's only for families and couples. No singles. I'm really sorry, but my grandfather always ran things that way, and he was right. It's quieter and less trouble. I've got a reputation to keep up. A lot of my campers are senior citizens, and they get nervous so easily. Please don't take this personally. I'm sure *you* wouldn't cause any trouble."

The disappointment that darkened his eyes twisted her resolve. He really seemed let down. "I understand, Agnes. I've put you in an embarrassing spot. Please don't worry. I approve of your rules."

"I apologize. I mean it."

"Your grandfather is . . . deceased?" he asked carefully.

She nodded. "He died a couple of months ago. He was in town doing some Latin research at the library, and he had a heart attack."

"I can hear the grief in your tone. How awful for you to lose him."

"I miss him," she admitted, and looked away, feeling vulnerable and distraught for many reasons, not just Grandpa's death.

"You ran this place together?"

"Yeah. When I was little he taught me everything he knew about horses. When I came back here five years ago, he made me a partner and gave me my father's old room. He was getting a little frail. I cooked for him and kept out of the way when his girlfriends came to visit."

"Girlfriends?"

She smiled. "Grandpa was popular with the senior set. He called them his gray foxes."

"And he studied Latin? He sounds fascinating."

Aggie nodded again. "He loved books. Funny, a grizzled old horse rancher and retired army captain, and he could speak Latin. It was like living with a retired Roman cavalry officer. Grandpa was unique."

She was silent, looking up at John thoughtfully and wondering how he'd managed to loose such personal information. And after she'd told him to hit the road.

"I'm sorry about the campground," she repeated. "Really."

"Sssh. I appreciate your concern, but there's no harm done." He had a subdued but understanding expression on his face. "If you could recommend another camping area I'd be grateful."

"Sure." Aggie reminded herself that there were too many strange coincidences about him—his being English and a medieval history buff. Fumbling with her bandanna, she pulled it off and twisted it in her hands. She didn't need the worry. Or the temptation to confide in him about the books. Too much was at stake.

"Could I help you feed your mares?" he asked. "I enjoy working with horses."

Aggie was relieved by the change of subject. "Sure!"

She smiled up at him, lost herself in his gaze for a second, then turned her attention to gathering her hair at the nape of her neck and tying it with the bandanna. "You must have been around horses a lot. You ride like an expert."

He chuckled, the warm, deep sound pulling at her blood. "Many years ago I was an alternate on the British equestrian team. I nearly made it to the Olympics." At her astonishment, he chuckled. "But 'nearly' is nothing to brag about."

"Of course it is! I can imagine how much competition there was to become an alternate. You must have been wonderful!"

He shrugged. "It was a long time ago. I was barely out of Oxford."

"Oxford? Now I'm even more impressed."

"It's a college, like any other."

"Right. And Van Gogh was just a one-eared painter."

"You're very sweet." He looked at her with a mixture of charm and intrigue that made it difficult to remember why she wanted him to leave. His hazel eyes could be so vibrant. "Agnes, would you go out to dinner with me this evening? Anyplace you'd like. I don't know St. Augustine. You choose."

"I have to work. It's Thursday, isn't it?" She stopped to think, embarrassed at her confusion. He'd turned her brain to sand. "Yeah, Thursday. I'm a bartender at the Conquistador Pub, Thursdays to Sundays."

"Agnes, you're a very difficult woman to charm." His teasing was mild. This man didn't sulk. "But I respect your hard work. Would you be annoyed if I dropped by the pub tonight? If you're in the mood, we could go to an all-night diner after you finish your shift."

"I don't finish until two A.M."

"I could swear I'm not bowling you over."

"You're only passing through. I don't get involved with tourists. I don't date very much, period."

He clasped his chest. "It's bad enough to fail at winning your heart, but now I can't even console myself! Couldn't you have told me you're devoted to another man? You have to be faithful to your one true love? Otherwise you'd give in to your desperate desire for me?"

Aggie laughed and started toward the pasture. "Look at it this way. I'm faithful to my bank balance, and it doesn't approve of me taking time off to play."

"But I'm very serious about my playing. My work is play, you know. Model airplanes, model cars—toys for grown-ups. I could teach you to play as if it were a business. You wouldn't have to feel guilty." She kept walking, shaking her head at his nonsense, and laughing. "Wait!" he called in an exasperated voice. "I'll change clothes and come with you."

"I don't know where the gals are this morning. They're usually standing out here looking hungry by now."

While he went back in the barn she stood by the pasture gate, staring across the flat, grassy expanse bordered by the forest of pines. Their conversation had left her breathless. Maybe there wouldn't be any harm in getting to know John Bartholomew better. Maybe those medieval manuscripts were making her too cautious. Why push a terrific man away without good reason?

But what if she missed him and felt miserable when he went back to England? No, thanks.

He returned wearing a blue T-shirt, wrinkled white shorts, and hiking boots similar to hers. "Onward, Lady Agnes," he said, opening the gate and sweeping a hand toward the pasture.

As they walked side by side down a path that skirted the woods, he mentioned his stranded Jeep. "If you'll drop me off at one of the rental-car places in town I'll take care of it." He cut his eyes at her mischievously. "Now here's an offer you can't refuse. Breakfast in town.

Even Wonder Woman must stop occasionally to nibble an egg and some muffins."

"Breakfast. Okay." She'd tell him good-bye afterward, and they'd go separate ways.

"Eureka! I've found the key to her heart!"

Aggie couldn't help laughing again. "It takes more than breakfast."

"Surely a lucky man or two has unlocked it."

Her humor faded. Shrugging, she said, "Well, I was married for a few years."

"Hmmm. I would have thought you'd have waited for someone irresistible."

"What makes you think I didn't?"

He flashed her a smile, but there was an edge to his dark gaze. "You'd still be married, if he were irresistible."

"Could be that he was irresistible at first, you know."

"No, by definition, 'irresistible' doesn't fade away."

She made an amused sound of disgust. "I have my doubts about your definition. It sounds convenient."

"But it's true."

"Okay, wise guy, then he wasn't irresistible. Satisfied?" She bent down as they talked, wrenched a sharp frond off a palmetto plant, and poked him in the arm. "Take that."

He sighed. "I don't joust with ladies. Go ahead, wound me. I suffer gallantly."

"Courage, thy name is Bartholomew." She tossed away the frond and shoved her hands in her shorts pockets. It was too easy to like his laid-back teasing. He was so comfortable with himself that he made her feel comfortable too.

"What did you do before you came here to live?" he asked, reaching out to take her elbow for a moment when she stumbled on a rock. He performed the little service without looking at her, then let go of her elbow as if such niceties were commonplace.

Aggie glanced at him anxiously. His gentlemanly attentions were so formal that she ought to make fun of him. Get real, she ought to say. Don't you know that chivalry is a joke?

"Thank you," she said.

"Hmmm?" He looked at her as if he couldn't imagine what was worth thanking him for. Aggie smiled at him while a warm sense of pleasure rose in her chest. She shook her head. "You were asking me a question. What I did before I came here. Well, I was married, as I said."

"That's not something you do, that's something you are. 'When a match has equal partners, then I fear not.' Aeschylus. Fifth century."

"Greek philosophers ought to watch a little *Divorce Court* on TV. They wouldn't be so sure, then."

John clucked his tongue. "What a stubborn woman you are!"

"Okay, so here are the facts. I was married, and I was an actress. I pretended I was happy."

"An actress? Really?"

"No, not really. I was a child actress who grew up and grew *out*." She gestured toward her breasts. "And I lost my career. Not that it was a brilliant career, anyway."

"Tell me more!"

She shrugged. "I was a cute baby, a cute kid, a cute tomboy, and a cute teenager. My specialty was playing rebellious little sisters. But then I hit adulthood. Nobody wants a twenty-year-old tomboy with more curves than an hourglass. I never said I was much of an actress, but dammit, I made a *great* TV kid."

"What kind of work did you do?"

She broke her stride long enough to give him a small curtsy before going on. "I was Meg for three years on *The Jones Family* and Sally for five years on *Pop's World*. These weren't classics. Every TV critic in the country made fun of them, but they were hits."

"Critics have no taste."

"Oh, in this case, they were right." She clasped her chest dramatically. "But my real claim to fame was commercials. Even my baby behind was captured on film for all time. I was the Sweetheart Shampoo baby." She made her voice wicked. "I was a show-off at an early age."

"You're making it all sound too easy. It takes talent to be that successful."

"No, it takes having the right 'look' and very greedy parents."

Before he could ask for more on that subject, she trotted off the path and into the pasture, then put two fingers in her mouth and gave an ear-piercing whistle. She called to John, "We'll either get horses or taxis!"

He walked through the tall grass toward her, smiling. The morning sunshine backlit him with golden light, playing beautifully on the olive tone of his skin. There must be an exotic-looking Moor or two in his ancestry, Aggie thought, groaning silently at such whimsy. A Moorish ancestor. Right. Only about seven centuries ago.

She'd been doing too much research on medieval history. Her mind wouldn't let go of it. Of Sir Miles of Norcross. Of John Bartholomew. They were tangled in her thoughts.

"Show me how you do that," he ordered, stopping in front of her. "That whistle could call spirits from their sleep. Or at least give them an earache."

*Call spirits from their sleep.* Why did he always say things that unnerved her? It was uncanny because of her ridiculous, overstimulated imagination.

"Like this. Make a circle, and leave a little space between your thumb and forefinger. Put them between your lips and clamp down." She showed him. "Pwull tight and bwow."

He tucked his chin and leaned forward, studying her lips intently. "I beg your pardon? What?"

Aggie's stomach tingled. She felt silly, but more than that she felt reckless. Suddenly she was aware of the undercurrent of arousal in her body, the sensitivity of her breasts, the delicious pressure deep in her belly, the tenderness of her lips as she scrubbed a finger across them.

"Pull tight and blow," she repeated, her breath short. She put her finger and thumb back into her mouth, turned her head, and demonstrated. The whistle was an airy, weak imitation of the first one. "Damn."

"Problems?" he inquired.

"Temporary loss of air pressure. You try." She touched her lips, showing him the exact placement.

His dark brows raised in watchful study, he copied her. His fingertips were large and the skin coarse-looking, the kind that could tantalize a woman's skin. He rubbed his thumb and finger over the cleft in his lips. "Right here?"

"Put them inside."

"Here?"

"That's fantastic . . . fine. That's fine."

"I doubt I have your sense of touch. Too much thick skin."

"That's what happens when you work with airplane glue all the time, I guess.

"Blow," she instructed shakily. "Go ahead."

He turned his head and made a loud but inarticulate sound. Grinning, he faced her again. "I sound like an air hose with a kink in it."

"Your pucker's all wrong. You need practice."

"Are you saying that my lips are out of condition?"

"Oh, I'm sure they get plenty of exercise. Maybe the wrong kind, though."

"You'll have to be specific. I'm confused."

"Uh-huh. I can see how confused you are."

"Could you mean this sort of exercise?" He stepped closer and angled his head downward, so that his mouth was near hers. His voice dropped to a throaty tease. "The kind where sincerity is more important than skill?"

Some devilish impulse took control of her voice. "You'll have to be more specific," she mimicked in an English accent. "I'm confused."

"You're a coy one, my lady."

"Look who's talking."

"Let's stop talking all together."

He kissed her and she couldn't move, couldn't raise a hand to push him away or a foot to step backward. He enchanted her with only the taste and firmness of his mouth, and she clasped her hands behind her to keep from reaching for him.

So he reached for her. While his mouth played slowly over hers, tugging at her lips and opening them only enough to provoke her, he carefully slid one arm around her waist. She was stiff with resistance until his hand fanned across her lower back, rubbing circles on her spine through the soft T-shirt. Aggie sighed and her body relaxed on some natural inner cue that she couldn't control.

Sometimes she forgot how lonely she was, and how much she wanted a man in her life. Now John made all that emptiness gather into a glowing center as hot as the Florida sun.

"Agnes, it's all right to play," he whispered. "One second more, please. Would you mind if I held you closer?"

Did men still ask permission for these things? She couldn't remember any in her experience. She looked into his patient eyes and knew this was a first for her. And suddenly, she didn't want to ruin it.

"Yes, I'd like that," she whispered.

She stepped into the tightening circle of his arm and slowly raised her hands to his shoulders. The feel of his hard chest and stomach merging with hers was as delightful as she'd expected. A warm morning breeze curled around them, and she couldn't tell if she was swaying with it or dizzy from emotion.

She touched his lips with the tip of her tongue and he tickled hers in return. Aggie half expected him to crush her mouth and slide deep inside; after the invitation she'd given, most men would take charge. Instead he began to kiss her face. One of his hands rose to her hair, pulled the bandanna down, and stroked the tangled strands. He cupped her head so that his thumb lay against her cheek, then caressed it.

Holding her that way, he kissed her nose, her chin, her cheeks, and finally her forehead, even feathering her lips over the swollen spot.

"I've never been married," he told her, putting his head beside hers so that he could kiss her ear. "Because I've never met a woman who was irresistible. Until you. I hardly know you, but I know that you're unique."

Distrust and surprise surged through her. She drew her head back. "Why do men think that women will do anything at the mention of the M word?"

"The M word?"

"Marriage. Do men think it's some kind of aphrodisiac? Is mentioning it supposed to make women feel flattered? Is hinting about it supposed to change a casual kiss into something serious? Or maybe give a gal an excuse to let her guard down?" She looked over his shoulder as if addressing someone else. "'But mother, he was so nice! Before he turned into a jerk, he mentioned marriage!'" She shot a cold look at John. "There was no need for you to overdo your flattery. Be honest."

He stepped back just enough to glare down at her easily. "What ugly suspicions you have." His voice was hard. "Your husband must have hurt you terribly for you to be so cruel to me."

"So cruel to you?"

"Yes. Isn't it possible that men get hurt as easily as

women do? Did I deserve that painful little whipping? It would have done no harm for you to accept my compliments and keep your doubts to yourself, then give me a chance to prove my sincerity."

Her mouth open, she gazed at him in surprise. He was genuinely hurt. But he didn't retreat behind pride and anger, he admitted that he was wounded. "Oh, come on, you're no kid, and I'm sure you have a long history with women. Don't tell me you haven't used that 'marriage' line before."

"Why is it that women think they're the only romantic ones?" He let go of her but took her hands, holding them firmly. Because he didn't stalk away with masculine arrogance, he made her even sorrier she'd upset him.

"Women have more to lose," she countered, jerking his hands a little.

"Nonsense. Don't play feminine games, and I won't play masculine ones. Your accusation was directed straight at me. Admit it."

She trembled. "Okay. You say I'm unique. Well, I say you're unique. I don't know how to deal with you. If I'm suspicious and mean, it's because you scare the hell out of me."

"Good enough. That announces the problem boldly, and I approve. Be frightened of me, if you must, but don't accuse me of sins I've never committed."

"Let's pretend this kiss didn't happen. And I apologize for my ugly attitude. Good enough? Now we're back where we started—two strangers who don't have as much in common as you think. But you're a nice man. I mean that."

"Nice" was an understatement. She moved back and squeezed his hands to signal that she wanted him to release her. His expression somber, he opened his fingers and let her hands slip away. His dignity gave him power and made her feel foolish. "We have a great deal in common, Agnes. And if you think I can forget the feel of you in my arms or the sweetness of your mouth, you sadly underestimate yourself. Even if it was centuries ago that I'd kissed you, I'd still remember how lovely it was."

Her knees turned to rubber. Something was going on here that she didn't understand. *I could have kissed you centuries ago.*

"Thank you for the compliment," she said weakly. "Now if you don't mind, I have horses to feed, if I can find them."

He nodded. "Practical matters first. Yes, you're right."

As they hunted for the mares she covered her troubled thoughts by telling him the horses' bloodlines and the cost of breeding each to a quality stallion. Her grandfather had worked for decades to build up his stock, and with enough hard work of her own, Aggie hoped to make the little ranch a big name among quarter-horse patrons.

John asked pleasant questions and acted as though the scene in the pasture had never occurred. Aggie knew she'd never forget it.

As they rounded the peninsula of forest that hid the rest of the pasture from view, John suddenly grasped her arm. Aggie whirled toward him, ready to fight another of his invasions on her common sense.

But his face was grim, and he pointed toward a distant stretch of fence. The solitary oak that had been a favorite shade spot for Hamilton livestock over the years now lay in the jumble of boards and hog wire that had been a good thirty-foot section of fence.

"This explains why the mares didn't come up this morning," he noted.

Aggie groaned. She suspected where the mares had gone, and she knew she was going to need John's help to get them back.

She needed him too much now.

# *Three*

Okay, there were good reasons to have John Bartholomew around, Aggie admitted. The man could probably charm sand crabs out of the sand. With any luck, he'd make Ida Roberts act nearly human. On the other hand, if Ida was as cranky as ever, she would at least divert Aggie's attention from the awkward problem of having John Bartholomew around.

She steered her truck down a two-lane road bordered by gnarled live oaks and scrub pine. John seemed to relish this new opportunity to make himself indispensable. His patience was seductive.

"I can't imagine why this lady would dislike you," he said abruptly, as if he'd been pondering the question for some time. He had his head up and his eyes half shut. The wind ruffled his thick, chocolate-colored hair. He looked content. "You don't seem to dislike her. And you're very good-natured."

"You weren't thinking that back in the pasture."

"I was thinking that you're too cautious, but that's no crime. Even if it's misdirected, in my case."

"We met less than twenty-four hours ago. I think I'm being reckless, not cautious."

"For kissing me? No. Deep down you know I'm wonderful and we're going to have a wonderful time together."

She laughed to take the edge off her next words. "This isn't a beach movie and we're not having a summer romance. So don't expect any clambakes."

"You can't insult me," he insisted, his tone droll, "because I have no idea what you're talking about."

"Now come on, you can't tell me you never saw a Frankie and Annette flick. What are you—thirty-something years old, right? And you never saw *Beach Blanket Bingo* when you were a kid? Even an English kid oughta know about Frankie and Annette."

"I had an unusual upbringing."

He spoke with a hard edge in his voice. She glanced at him curiously, but couldn't analyze his shuttered expression. She pondered what she knew about him. He'd attended one of England's most pretigious colleges, been an alternate on the Olympic equestrian team, and was the heir to a successful family business. That spelled big money and blue blood.

"You must have gone to private schools," she prodded. "Pretty strict and traditional, from what I've heard. Nobody wasted time watching TV or going to silly movies."

He was silent for so long that she wondered if he'd heard her. "Something like that," he said finally.

His voice was so subdued, she felt protective of him. Aggie gritted her teeth. He was two hundred-plus pounds of muscular, rugged handsomeness, with a face that looked as if it had been molded by intense passions. He was educated and successful. Protection was the last thing he needed. So she'd treat him like a testy stallion with a sore leg—she'd be sympathetic, but watch out for his kick.

"Aw, never mind about Frankie and Annette," she told him. "You didn't miss anything important. I shouldn't have teased you."

"You can tease me all you want." He exhaled, as if relieved, and draped his arm along the back of the seat. Then he twirled a finger into a strand of her ponytail. "But I'll tease back."

"So let me tell you more about Ida Roberts," she said quickly. "She had a feud with my grandpa, and I inherited it."

"A feud about what?"

"Ducks. Really ugly ducks."

"I beg your pardon?"

"Domestic ducks. Mixed breeds. Big ones. With no manners and nonstop appetites. Whenever Grandpa's horses got out and visited Ida's place, they became hostages in the duck war. Ida locked mares in her pasture and refused to give them back."

"What did he have to do?"

"Let her call him names." She turned onto a private drive lined with graceful mimosa trees. Their feathery green fronds reached toward the truck. John held his hand out the window and let them brush his fingertips. But he kept his other hand lightly twined in her hair. She could barely feel it, but every inch of her body knew it was there.

"Is that all she does? Call people names?" John asked.

"Usually. Don't be surprised if she calls you 'a snake from a scum pond,' or something even more disgusting."

The truck's wheels made crackling noises on the drive's crushed-shell surface. John's deep chuckle added a smooth baritone note, relaxed and confident. "A snake from a scum pond. How rude," he said lightly. "Tell me what else to expect."

"You'll see. Don't get mad. She loves a fight. She used to provoke Grandpa until he'd have to come home and take an extra blood-pressure tablet."

"You're certain she has your horses?"

Aggie nodded. "They cut across the edge of the marshes

to her backyard. Ida only has two acres, with half of it fenced in. They head straight for her pasture to see Pogo."

"Pogo?"

"A midget four-footed Romeo. The Napoleon of the pony set. Small, sexy, and overconfident. The gals think he's fabulous. And he, of course, thinks they're right."

"Is he a threat? Any chance of an illicit love affair between Pogo and one of your princesses?"

"Not unless somebody gives him a box to stand on."

John's hearty, astonished laugh made her grin, while at the same time she kicked herself for being so blunt. "Excuse me," she added. "I used to be more delicate. Now I spend too much time in the barn."

"It's a pleasant place, your barn."

"It's better with company. I mean . . . oh, hell. Open mouth, insert foot. You know what I'm trying to say."

"I wish you meant it the way it sounded."

She stomped on the accelerator. He was helping her dig herself in too deep, but she was doing most of the shoveling. "So let me finish telling you about Ida and the ducks. People bring the ducks to Ida's pond. Ida loves the ducks. I don't know why, because they are, without a doubt, the nastiest, ugliest ducks in the known world. These are escapees from Easter baskets or something. No one's sure. They hatch little ducks like crazy and take over every lake, pond, and puddle of fresh water. There's a battle between people who want the ducks left alone and people who want the ducks roasted over an open spit. Grandpa was a roaster."

John was laughing silently. "So he and Ida clashed?"

"Yeah. Locals would sneak into the campground with ducks they'd captured. They dumped them in our lake. Grandpa would round up the ducks and sell them to an alligator zoo over in Ocala."

"Where they enjoyed long, happy lives as companions for the alligators, of course."

"*Of course.*"

"And Mrs. Roberts objected?"

"Yeah."

"She's not selling roast duck on the sly, is she?"

"Oh, no. She's a vegetarian."

"Good thing she's not an alligator."

Aggie began grinning. Suddenly, because John was with her, she wasn't dreading Ida's tirade anymore. "I'd rather deal with a gator. A kinder bite than Ida's."

John laughed again. She was beginning to love the sound. A giddy wildness was growing inside her. "And you?" he asked. "Where did you stand in the duck war between Mrs. Roberts and you late grandfather?"

"I think Ida's an impractical fool for thinking she can give every duck in the country a permanent home, but I sort of hated for the ducks to become alligator munchies. Don't get me wrong, I'm no softie where ducks are concerned. I can't afford to be. I've got my own tail feathers to worry about."

"It's all right to be a softie at heart, Agnes. You love animals, even ducks. I think that's marvelous."

His admiration made her tingle, even though she suspected it was only flattery. Well, she could use some flattery, she told herself—as long as she enjoyed it but didn't believe it.

"My mother's parents were Quakers," she told John. "I used to visit them up in Pennsylvania when I was little. That is, whenever I wasn't working out in California. I really loved their farm. They weren't sentimental about their animals, but they respected them. They had a live-and-let-live attitude toward things."

"Your mother was a Quaker too?"

Aggie chewed the inside of her mouth for a moment. "Not when it interfered with what she wanted. No. Mom didn't get along with her folks." She made her voice breezy and changed the subject. "So maybe those kindhearted Quaker instincts jumped a generation, and I got them."

She made a disgusted sound at her whimsical explanation and realized that being with John made her think about who and what she was—and how different her background was from his.

"Tell me about your parents," he prompted. "Are they both living?"

"Oh, let's stop talking about my family," she said lightly. "Take my word for it. You and I don't have much in common. When it comes to family histories, you got the Broadway production and I got the road company."

"And we speak different languages, too, because I'm bewildered again."

"My parents weren't a class act. I'm ashamed of them. Enough said."

"*Agnes.*" His voice was almost angry. "What do their problems have to do with you? You're very special and have nothing to be ashamed of." He reached over and took one of her hands from the steering wheel, brought it to his mouth, kissed it forcefully, then placed it back on the wheel. "Enough said," he mimicked, but with a strained tone.

Aggie shivered with a mixture of surprise, curiosity, and poignant affection. Searching for something nonchalant to say, she could only toss back, "Well, I'm proud of being part Quaker." She exhaled shakily. The mood in the truck's cab reminded her of the energized air before last night's storm. "So anyhow, now you understand about the duck war."

"You're not exactly a Quaker." John cleared his throat. "Under these circumstances, I'd call you a *Quacker.*"

She sputtered, cast a sidelong look at his suppressed smile, and burst into giggles. "A Quacker. Yeah."

"You secretly love ducks," he continued, his voice fiendish. "I'm sure of it. I'll tell Mrs. Roberts that we've come to take a few dozen back with us."

"Do it and I'll twist your beak so hard you can't peck worms for a month."

He chuckled. "How dare you threaten my pecker. I take great pride in it. I won't let you stroke it, if you keep talking that way."

For a second she was stunned. Then, fighting a smile, she asked, "John, in England, what's the definition of 'pecker'?

He arched one brow and studied her as if she were asking a trick question. "It's something a bird pecks with," he answered cautiously.

"No other meaning, huh?"

"What is it in your—oh, *Agnes*, I can see by the look on your face! Is it what I think it is?"

She nodded fervently. Her giggles became soft, breathless gulps of merriment.

John groaned. "I apologize."

"Your beak is safe from me."

"Agnes, I would *never* make a crude joke like that on purpose."

As she guided the truck through the magnolia trees in front of Ida's white cottage, she was clutching her mouth with one hand and trying to stop snickering. It didn't help that there were ducks everywhere—sitting on the cottage's roof, perched in the trees, pecking around in the flower beds, and sunning themselves on Ida's new compact car.

"See, John? It's a Duck-o-Rama!" She couldn't resist adding, in a choked voice, "The little peckers are *everywhere*."

He leaned back, laughing and shaking his head. "I'm glad you aren't upset by my slip of the tongue."

"Upset? John, you've gotta be one of the last gentlemen on the face of the planet. I could put you on display and sell tickets to millions of adoring women."

He tucked his chin and looked at her with a breathtaking combination of invitation and good humor. "My beak is available only for private audiences."

Aggie giggled harder as he dissolved into his wonderful baritone chuckles again. At that moment a dozen mottled, black and white ducks chose to scurry out from behind a toolshed and dodge the truck's front bumper. Aggie slammed on the brakes. They hissed and ran, their wings spread. Flapping and waddling, they hurried to a pond surrounded by oaks several hundred feet behind the house. The pond was already overcrowded with feathered swimmers.

Aggie screeched then slumped in the seat, chortling. "I won't get out of here without causing a feathered frenzy. I just know it."

John prodded her shoulder with one finger and smiled wickedly. "It's a good thing they ducked."

His prim attitude compounded the absurdity and brought her giggles to an uncontrollable level. They now had a mind of their own. She saw Ida on the porch, frowning at her, and swallowed hard, fighting for calm. John tapped her shoulder again. "Really, Agnes, do be serious." He made his voice very solemn and aristocratic. "Agnes, that very stern-looking lady on the porch thinks we're daffy."

"I'll be Daffy, and you be Donald."

"Aren't they cartoon ducks?"

"Yeah."

"But aren't they *male* cartoon ducks?"

"Yeah. So?"

"But then I couldn't kiss you again. I'm not that kind of duck."

She threw the floor shift into park, stamped weakly on the emergency brake, cut the engine, then hugged the wheel and nearly yelped with laughter. It was the nuttiness of the whole morning, her nervousness over John and the medieval books, and a long-lost need to be silly. Obviously he intended to reduce her to a pile of hiccups.

He leaned close and asked sternly, "Are you about to lay an egg?" Aggie rolled against him, holding her stomach with both hands and gasping. From the corner of one squinted eye she saw Ida march down the porch's wooden steps. Her gray hair, twisted into an upthrust knot at the crown of her head, bobbed with an anger of its own as she strode across the sandy yard, and her bright-pink tennis shoes made forceful impressions. Her print work dress sucked in and out between her knees.

John whispered in Aggie's ear, "You didn't tell me that Mrs. Roberts is nearly two meters tall and probably outweighs me. If she becomes violent, I'll be injured protecting myself."

"You? W-what about *me*? What do you charge for bodyguard services?"

"For duck cases? I don't know. I'll have to *bill you* later."

"Bill me. Agggh." Crying with laughter, Aggie rested her head in the crook of his neck and pounded her knees. "Ida w-will never f-forgive me," she said between gasps.

Ida stormed up to the truck and stuck her face in the open window. "What the hell is your problem?"

Aggie swallowed gulps of air and sat up. She felt like a roller coaster balanced at the top of a hill. One look at Ida's quivering topknot, and her lungs contracted again with spasms of laughter. The roller coaster plunged downward and all she could do was hang on for the ride.

She made a sputtering sound and shook her head. There had only been a few times, as a child working with professional adult actors, when she'd been this broken up by someone's sly humor. John had undone her with more than silly teasing. He made her feel comfortable, natural, and safe. She was ripe for relief from stress. He seemed to sense it.

"Miss Hamilton was hit in the head last night," he told Ida solemnly. He extended a hand across Aggie's lap and out the truck's window to her. "How do you do, madame? I'm John Bartholomew. A friend of Miss Hamilton's."

"I'm not interested in shaking your hairy-ape hand." Ida stared at Aggie, who looked back helplessly, choking on giggles and contorting her face to keep them in. "You better not be laughing at me, you redheaded cow."

Aggie's eyes widened. "M-moo. M-moo." She covered her face and turned to bury her head in John's big shoulder again. Her heels drummed on the floorboard.

He stroked her hair. "Madame, she's not herself."

"I couldn't care less if she was a Mutant Ninja Toad! Her stud-crazy horses are locked up in my pasture with my Pogo, and I intend to keep 'em until I get good and ready to let 'em go!"

"T-turtle," Aggie corrected. "Mutant Ninja T-turtle." John curved one arm around her head and clamped a hand over her mouth. She began laughing against his palm. It was a wide, hard, sexy palm, she decided. She made tiny quacking sounds into it. She felt his chest quivering against her bowed head.

He cleared his throat. "On behalf of Miss Hamilton, I apologize for any inconvenience."

"Forget about your slime-licking apologies! I don't want them! I thought I was done with the Hamiltons! But it looks like I've traded the old goat for a young nanny!"

Aggie convulsed. "Baaah." John's hand muffled the sound.

"What did you call me?" Ida asked.

John intervened quickly. "Miss Hamilton wants you to know that she's not going to follow in her grandfather's footsteps. Any ducks which are deposited at her lake in the future will be turned over to you. Agnes wants the ducks to be happy."

"I don't trust her! She's exactly like her fish-gutted grandfather!"

"I hope so," Aggie managed to say, twisting her mouth away from John's hand. For a moment she could only make small moaning noises of amusement and shiver with restraint. "He didn't like selling the ducks for alligator snacks, but he knew that you were already overrun with them. And you wouldn't let him donate any money or feed for their upkeep. He felt sorry for you. So do I."

"You pig-livered cat! I didn't need sympathy from Sam Hamilton, and I don't need sympathy from you—a has-been actress who was married to a drug dealer!"

Aggie gave another soft snuffle of laughter, but the humor died inside her. She sat up, avoiding John's gaze, and looked wryly at the irate Ida. "Even has-been actresses feel sorry for somebody like you."

"Get your mares out of my pasture and keep 'em away from here!"

Growing somber now, Aggie said firmly, "Can do. I'm sorry they bothered you, Ida. And I'm sorry you have such a mean mouth."

"I'll 'mean-mouth' you, you Technicolor tramp. Why don't you sell your ranch to somebody who knows how to be a good neighbor? Go back to Holly-weird and walk around half-nekkid in another trashy TV movie! Uncover some more of your talent, 'cause you sure can't do anything else right!"

"Madame," John interjected abruptly, in a voice that had become cold and devilish, "if you don't stop making insulting speeches, I'll get out of this truck, come 'round to your side, and kiss you until you turn purple."

The bizarre threat silenced Ida as nothing else ever had. Her mouth hung open. She took several stiff steps back from the truck, staring at John the whole time. "Don't you dare, you shark-faced hellion!"

"I will, madame. I promise. And if you don't go into your house immediately, I'll demand you apologize to Miss Hamilton. In fact, I think I'll demand it right now. An apology, madame. This second."

Ida shook her fists at him, "Why, you—" John started to open the truck door. Ida shrieked, then turned and bustled into her house, slamming the screen door and then the wooden one. Aggie watched the door quiver and all the way across the yard could hear the lock click.

She frowned pensively and swiveled her gaze back to John. "I've never heard a more creative or more gallant threat. It was incredible." She searched his eyes and tried to determine his thoughts. Her stomach had ice in it. "Thank you."

"He took one of her hands and lifted it to his mouth. His lips touched the back of it as if her skin were silk. "At your service, fair lady."

"Look, you can drop that 'lady' stuff."

"No." He raised his head and studied her firmly. "What's next, Lady Agnes?"

He wasn't going to ask about the things Ida had said. Aggie's throat burned with emotion. He wasn't even going to look curious. She could have kissed him again.

"I'll ride Valentine. She's the one you rode last night. She's the boss. The others will follow her. Will you drive the truck back to my place?"

"Certainly."

Aggie got out and reached into the truck's bed for the bridle she'd tossed there. "Insurance. I don't want to go home at a gallop."

John came to her side and took the truck keys she offered. He looked down at her with so much reassurance in his expression that she felt like crying. One second laughing like a hyena, the next on the verge of tears. She was coming unglued.

If he noticed, he didn't say so. "You could use help mending that fence this afternoon."

Her shoulders sagged. "No. There's not a damned thing I can give you in return for that much work. Not money, not a good time, not even a good meal, because I'm a worse cook than I was an actress."

"You better stop before you insult me, Agnes."

She studied the hard glint in his eyes then nodded. "I want you to understand that I'm too busy to go on vacation with you. I hate for you to waste even one day of your trip on me."

"Working on your ranch would be different from anything I do at home. I'd enjoy myself if you'd stop worrying about it."

"Gee, maybe when I've known you for a long time—like maybe a week—I'll feel foolish for feeling uncomfortable."

"Time has nothing to do with it," he said, his voice becoming gruff. He put a hand on her shoulder and squeezed lightly. His expression was troubled as he watched her. "A day, a week, a decade, a hundred decades—what difference does it make? We have all the time we need."

She wanted to ask, For what? but she was afraid. She might like his answer.

"I'll help you with the fence," he repeated. "After we feed your horses, see about my Jeep, and have breakfast. All right?"

"All right."

"And then, if you'll tell me where to find another campground, I'll move out of your barn." He studied her expression carefully. "If you still want me to leave."

She struggled in a silent war with herself. Thirty-one years of hard experience said to keep him as far away as possible; the past few hours of intense companionship told her to hang on to him for dear life.

Aggie clasped the sore bump on her forehead. "I'm still scrambled. Let me think about it."

"That's all I ask, Agnes." He looked pleased.

Nothing was going the way it should. She was pleased too.


John traded his rented Jeep for another one, then let Agnes buy him breakfast at a diner overlooking Matanzas Bay and the historic section of St. Augustine, where the massive, gray Castillo de San Marcos still loomed over the bay's entrance, as it had since the 1600s. He loved the feel of the city, with its Spanish styles and aging Victorian opulence. Having grown up in a city where the past was a living force, he couldn't scoff at Agnes Hamilton's affection for her own city.

He liked listening to her chirpy Southern voice as she told him about local history. He liked seeing her eyes light up with pleasure. What was so wrong with that? The scene this morning with that crone, Ida Roberts, had made him feel like snuggling Agnes inside his arms and promising that he'd never let anyone call her names again. Even if she had possession of his inheritance, and even if she had a reputation as notorious as his own—and might have been given it unfairly, he was beginning to believe—Agnes deserved to enjoy herself. He was willing to admit that it thrilled him to make her smile.

"How did you get those scars on your knuckles?" she asked, pointing to the network of fine white lines on his right hand.

"They're sports-related," he said vaguely.

"Let me guess. I know! Fencing. I can picture you doing an Errol Flynn routine with one of those long thin swords."

"I may not have heard of Annette and Frankie, but I do know about Errol Flynn. It wasn't quite like that."

"But you got those scars in fencing tournaments. I knew it." She nodded sagely. "And how'd you get that little oval scar on the front of your neck?"

John stared at her in dismay. Why not tell her the kind of story she wanted to hear? "I splattered hot oil on myself during a business trip to the Orient. I was in an antiques shop examining oil lamps. I collect them."

Agnes sighed in admiration. Exactly what she'd expected, her smile said. "Tell me more," she urged.

His stomach twisted with disgust. He'd never collected any kind of art or antiques, unless one considered cheap detective novels and photos of famous London criminals. His scars were from street fights.

She appeared to believe everything he said. Watching her prop her intelligent, rosy-cheeked face on one hand as she listened to him, never looking away, her beautiful eyes trying to trust him, did a nasty thing to his appetite. Guilt replaced it, poking him in the stomach until all he could swallow were sips of his weak American coffee and a few bites of fried egg.

She probably had his inheritance stashed somewhere, damn her. And she had to know it was stolen. Even though she wasn't the one who'd pilfered it during the war almost fifty years ago, she was the one who stood to benefit from the theft.

There was no reason to feel guilty for doing whatever it took to worm the truth out of her. Worm. He felt like a worm. Very well. So he could live with himself, anyway.

He remembered as a boy watching his father cheat at a card game with the stable hands. The manager of the Bennington stables getting drunk and cheating his own workers!

His father was despised by the men who worked for him, but they were too much in awe of him to complain to the estate's lord. They took out their frustrations by tormenting John. He'd learned to fight, to work harder than everyone else, and to dissect human nature.

Those skills had saved him from the streets. He'd earned sergeant's rank in the army. Then he'd gone to college, and by the time he turned twenty-five he was on his way to becoming a detective with Scotland Yard. Until last year, he'd been one of their best.

He'd played by the rules, and the rules had betrayed him. So this time he'd make up his own rules. Six months ago a London rare-book broker had tracked him down after being contacted by Sam Hamilton. John had listed his family's books in Scotland Yard's records of stolen art objects. The dealer had checked the records because the books Hamilton wanted him to sell were so valuable.

John wondered what would have happened if he'd come here then, while Sam Hamilton was still alive. At John's request, the dealer hadn't warned Hamilton. He'd told him that he needed to see the books before he agreed to represent them, and Hamilton refused.

John had planned to pay Hamilton a surprise visit, but then his life had come apart at the seams. Betrayal. Accusations that he'd taken bribes from the terrorist organizations he'd been assigned to infiltrate. A trial. A conviction. Three months in prison. The end of his career and reputation. And Sam Hamilton had died of a heart attack in the meantime.

After all that, getting the books from Agnes Hamilton ought to be a piece of cake. He wasn't going to let desire get in the way.

Let her believe he was some kind of knight in shining armor. Let her believe that lie.

# *Four*

By the time they began rebuilding the pasture fence that afternoon, John knew she wouldn't ask him to leave. He could see the gratitude and affection blazing behind her troubled blue eyes. John covered his guilty eyes with absurdly conservative black sunglasses to protect himself from her scorching attention and the semitropical sun. Her attention was hotter, no contest.

At first he made pleasant small talk when he wasn't cutting the oak apart with a chain saw. But she gave one-word answers and worked as swiftly as a lumberjack. A dangerous female lumberjack, John thought with exasperation. It was hell to concentrate on handling a chain saw when Agnes's peach-shaped rump strained against her shorts each time she bent over.

Her hands were covered in thick leather gloves, and perspiration shone like a crystal veneer on her face and arms as she chopped at small tree branches with a hatchet and carried off the big chunks that fell from the chain saw's whirring blade. She sucked her lower lip when she was concentrating hard, and she gave the tree limbs orders under her breath.

So many small things about her delighted him. It seemed silly to love the coconut scent of her suntan lotion, or enjoy her ferocious attitude toward the tree.

At any minute he expected her to wrap her arms around a thick limb and wrestle it. Soon her legs below her baggy brown shorts were stained with grime, bits of broken leaves, and thin pink scratches. She didn't seem to notice or care.

"Do you tackle all your work this way?" he asked finally. He let the chain saw idle, liking the raw power of it humming in his hands. When he looked up at Agnes he felt a similar humming inside him, just as unadorned and powerful, deep in his blood. She was a helluva fighter, his Agnes. His Agnes. Taking a breath to clear that notion from his thoughts, he watched her put a hand to her ear and shake her head.

He cut the saw's motor a little more and called cheerfully above the sound, "I'd like to see you in a garden taming thorny roses."

"You have a rose garden?" she yelled back as she dragged away a limb.

Damn. That kind of question forced him to do gymnastics with his answer. "Only a small garden. At my place in the city." John coughed. The only garden he had was the withered brown fern he'd left on the fire escape outside his flat's back door.

"You've got a town house?"

John cursed silently. More gymnastics. "Something like that."

She dropped the limb alongside others in a pile to be burned, then put her gloved hands on her hips and gave him and his vague answer a sardonic look. Her luscious hips, like her attitude, were provocative. John gunned the saw's engine and smiled at her.

"Keep sassing me, Mr. Bartholomew, and I'll jam your motor."

He turned the motor off, hoping to win a few more minutes of her entertaining conversation. "I never *sass* beautiful women who carry battle-axes."

She nodded and patted the hatchet, which she'd

hung from a tool belt around her waist. "Smart man." She went back to work, latching on to a new limb with both hands. "So you've got a London town house with a rose garden, huh? Where do you keep the yacht and the Rolls?"

"No yacht. And I drive an ordinary old car." That, at least, was entirely true.

"Let me guess. You look like a Ferrari man. Classy but not conservative."

He muttered under his breath and gave up. "That's me. A Ferrari. Sleek, fast, and powerful."

"I knew it!" She looked heavenward. "He says he drives 'an ordinary old car,'" she drawled wryly, shaking her head. "There *ain't* no such *thang* as an 'old Ferrari.' An old Ferrari is a classic Ferrari."

"Well, all right," he said, defeated. "It's a classic Ferrari."

"I know about Ferraris." She jerked a branch free and tossed it toward the pile. Her voice became somber, the playful drawl gone. "My dad had a couple. Used to let me cruise around Los Angeles in one, when I got my first driver's license. What a car!"

"Tell me more about your parents."

She shook her head and kept talking. "What year is your Ferrari?"

John considered her slowly. She wasn't ever going to tell him about her parents, he suspected. He knew why. He'd researched them along with her. Over the years they'd gambled away all the money she made in television, mismanaged her trust fund, and left her broke when her career faded. A year after she turned twenty-one they'd died in a car accident near Las Vegas.

He knew from personal experience how terrible growing up with irresponsible parents could be. He wished he could assure her he understood her shame.

"John?"

"Hmmm?" He blinked swiftly and tried to remember what she'd asked him.

"Your Ferrari. What model is it?"

He searched his mind for information on Ferraris. If she'd asked him about classic guns or knives, he could have told her volumes. But no. She wanted to chat about Ferraris! "It's one of those late-sixties models, I think."

"You don't know?"

"I never get a chance to drive it."

"You don't drive at all? Oh, I should have known! I bet you also have a big Mercedes sedan and a chauffeur. Right?"

This was an impossible conversation. John thought about simply dropping the chain saw, leaping over the tree trunk between him and Agnes, and kissing her until she stopped asking questions.

He began chuckling wearily. She'd probably take the hatchet to him.

Agnes shot him a puzzled look. "What's funny?"

"The way you're figuring out my lifestyle."

"Was I right about the car and chauffeur?"

"Close enough."

"You've got class. Yeah, I can see it."

John frowned. If this kindhearted bird saw where he really lived and what he drove, she'd definitely threaten him with the hatchet.

"Well, class isn't a matter of fine homes or cars," he told her. "For example, I think you look very classy right now. As if you should be sitting around a campfire in the mountains with a glass of wine in one hand."

Soft peals of laughter came from her. "You are a bonafide sweet-talkin' man."

"Is that good?"

"The jury's still out on it."

"I beg your pardon?"

"I haven't decided about you yet."

"Ah. Hmmm. When you start dropping the g's off your words and speaking with honey in your vowels, you sound dangerous."

"Yeah. It's a warnin' sign. Means you're hearing the real me."

He recalled the episodes of *The Jones Family* he'd watched at the television archives of a university here in the States. Checking out her background had been one of his first goals. The television comedy show had been awful, complete nonsense. But redheaded little Agnes, who couldn't have been more than eight or nine at the time, had been charming. Not a very good actress, but lovable.

"I assume you didn't speak with an accent when you worked in television," he said nonchalantly.

"No way. No casting agent in California wanted a kid with a drawl." She put a hand to her throat and drew her shoulders back formally, then spoke in a crisp, un-accented voice, exaggerating the sounds. "So I learned to e-nun-ci-ate and mod-u-late and speak like ev-er-y other me-di-ocre TV kid."

"Fascinating. You're a different person when you do that."

She shrugged, melted back into her casual self, and returned to the tree-limb attack. "I *was* a different person."

"But not me-di-ocre, I'm sure."

When she glanced at him uncertainly and frowned, he knew she was uncomfortable. "I have to get to my job at the pub in about two hours," she announced. "We better stop talking and fix this fence."

He nodded and went back to work. But he couldn't stop watching her, and he couldn't ignore the pleasant sense of friendship growing inside him. And it was great to feel his muscles tighten and flex smoothly. There was something primitive and exciting about working in partnership with Agnes, both of them sweating and straining around the fence posts, sharing the spring day and the singing insects and the warm, earthy scents of the grassy land.

He wished she weren't so intent on seeing him as a pampered London businessman. She would certainly have doubts about his elite background if he told her how to pull the hog wire tighter or why the posts would set better with a little more dirt around them. He wasn't supposed to know about those things.

He'd even had to pretend ignorance about the chain saw, looking solemn when she repeated the safety precautions several times. She didn't know that he'd grown up in a dingy flat over a stable and had spent his boyhood doing the filthiest, hardest work a stable manager's son could do.

As Agnes held hog wire against a post and he swung a hammer with what he hoped wasn't too much skill, a searing pinprick of pain stabbed the back of his thigh. "A bee!" Agnes called. Then he hit his thumb with the hammer.

The words he said could have made saltwater boil. The hardest man on the hardest street in London couldn't have expressed himself better. And since John had been that man during his career with Scotland Yard, what he said came naturally.

Agnes covered her mouth with both gloved hands and stared at him. He tossed the hammer aside and stuck his thumb between his lips. As he sucked it he cursed himself silently and tried not to grimace with the pain, aside from wanting to scratch the throbbing itch just under the edge of his shorts leg in back.

John gritted his teeth in a smile. "I apologize."

Then he realized, as he studied Agnes's crinkling eyes, that behind the gloves she was struggling not to laugh. "Don't," she said in a strangled voice. "I'm s-sorry, It's not f-funny." She made snuffling sounds behind the gloves.

"Agnes! How could you!"

"You're real. You're human and real." She lowered her hands and drew her face into a mask of control. "I've never heard a man sound quite so, uh, real, in my whole life. I'm glad. I thought you were too perfect to be true. I feel a whole lot more comfortable now."

"I'm glad you enjoyed it." He felt relieved and surprised.

She tugged her gloves off, reached over the half-mended fence, and grasped his injured hand carefully. She brought it close. Her smile disappeared and she made a sharp sound of sympathy. "I *am* sorry. This is terrible."

John looked at the blood around his thumbnail with secret appreciation. It was nice to have Agnes fuss over him. It was serving his purpose, making her care about him. And . . . oh, hell, it was just nice for its own sake.

"I'm sure I'll live," he said bravely.

"Come on, I've got antiseptic and stuff at the house."

"No, that would take too much time. I'm fine. Really."

"But you're going to bleed all over my pasture."

"No, only in this corner of it." He liked the cozy way her hands cupped his, and he pulled his hand away reluctantly. "I'll clean my thumb up a bit, and then we'll get back to work." He reached for the tail of his T-shirt."

"Wait. Don't." She chewed her lower lip for a second, then grumbled something mild under her breath and unbuckled her tool belt. After she let it drop she began unbuckling the slender leather belt that held up her shorts.

John eyed her askance. "This is an interesting form of first aid."

"You're a lucky man." But she only loosened the belt a few notches, so that her shorts slid down to the top of her hipbones and hung there in tantalizing jeopardy of falling farther. Her T-shirt covered her stomach, but John glimpsed white panties.

The panties were waist-high and demure. But the

jagged horizontal tear revealing her navel was fantastic.

"Nice style," he said, even though a gentleman ought to look away. For the moment, he had to be himself.

"Dogs got hold of them." Her rosy cheeks flushed red at the centers as she lifted her shirt's hem over one hip and quickly grabbed the panties' waistband. She ripped the thin, cottony material from the band down to parts unseen under her shorts.

John let his imagination fill in the details. "You're giving me your lingerie?" he inquired solemnly. "I'm honored."

"I'm giving you my old cotton drawers. There's a difference."

"Only in form, not in spirit."

"Don't get philosophical about my underwear." She tore the other side then turned her back. "Guess you can't see anything anyway, but I'm having an attack of modesty."

"Agnes, you're the dearest bundle of contradictions in the world. I can curse like a drunken sailor and you laugh, but now you're embarrassed about revealing an innocent bit of material."

"That's me," she said over one shoulder, while maneuvering privately with the front of her shorts. "A bundle of contradictions."

"A lovely mystery."

"Don't say I never gave you anything." She bent her head and fiddled with the panties she had pulled free. He heard ripping sounds. She tucked a wad of remnants into one of her back pockets as she pivoted and faced him again. "Gimme your thumb."

He held out his hand obediently and she wrapped a strip of soft, warm cotton material around it. She tore the end of the strip in two and twined the ends around his thumb and tied them. "I played a nurse's aide once on *Marcus Welby*. I knew it'd come in handy, someday."

John studied his oddly bandaged thumb in silence.

The desire coursing through his blood dismayed him. Wearing a strip of Agnes Hamilton's cotton underwear around his thumb shouldn't be the most erotic thing he'd ever had happen to him, considering the inventive women he'd known. He shouldn't be tingling as if she'd just stroked him all over and asked him to lie down in the tall grass with her.

"It's a wonderful job, Agnes," he said finally.

"You don't look happy. Is it too tight?"

"No, it's fine. Thank you." He stepped back and scooped up the hammer he'd dropped. "We better get back to work." She looked bewildered and a little hurt by his change of mood. "Hey, it's not every day that I share my—Never mind. That wasn't going to come out the way I meant it."

"Let's get on with fixing this fence."

"Sure."

Looking subdued and thoughtful, she retrieved her gloves from the ground. John watched her in worried silence. Suddenly, his plans were not nearly as simple or as selfish as he wanted them to be.


Aggie and John rocked in the ancient rocking chairs, whose joints creaked from many pleasant years of use and drank iced tea from quart-sized plastic cups she'd collected at fast-food restaurants. Nothing fancy, nothing threatening. She was happy having a few mindless, pleasant moments with John before she had to make a decision about him.

But he wouldn't give her the luxury. "I'll have to be going, if I'm to find another campground."

She laced her hands around the cartoon characters dancing on her tall cup. "You know it's not that simple," she muttered.

"Agnes?" When she lifted her head and looked at him defensively, she found regret in his eyes. "I'll be blunt then. I hope you'll change your mind and let me stay. There are a dozen sights I want to see in this part of Florida, and I can see them alone, while you're working." He paused, intense emotions flickering in his eyes as his gaze held hers. A quiver ran through her. "And I'll take any of your free time you can give me."

She set her cup on the floor and, feeling shaky, moved to the porch railing across from him. Leaning against it, she untied her sweaty bandanna, pulled it off, and ran a distracted hand through her tangled, damp hair. "I wish I had time to do all the tourist things with you. I'd love to. It'd be the kind of fun I haven't had in years. But I don't have the time, and I'm afraid you'll be disappointed if you stay here."

"Tell me what your days are like. Not unusual days, like this, but the ordinary ones."

"Remember? I said I write a few articles for one of the neighborhood newspapers?"

"Yes. I'm impressed."

"I'm no professional reporter. It's simple writing, but I'm good at it. I interview local people, take a few photos, then write the articles. I get ten bucks a story from the *Matanzas Bay Weekly News*." She smiled at the name and watched amusement gleam in his eyes too. "Tomorrow I'll be interviewing a man who builds model trains." She brightened suddenly. "John! Would you like to go with me when I see him? You can ask him questions that I'd never think of!"

"Model trains?" His blank look was puzzling. It disappeared before she could study it. He smiled quickly. "Yes, I'd love to help you. You see? You needn't take time off to entertain me. I'm not a guest, I'm a friend."

"A temporary friend," she corrected somberly. "Who'll be going back to England in a few weeks."

"Agnes, live in the present!"

"That's funny, coming from a man who loves medieval history."

He bounded to his feet more quickly and gracefully than such a large man should, startling her. Plunking his cup on the porch rail, he grasped her hands warmly. His skin was burnished from the afternoon in the sun, and he smelled pleasantly earthy. His walnut-dark hair shagged over his forehead in an untamed way that tempted her fingers, and his smile flashed white in contrast. The vibrant joy in his eyes made them sparkle. "I love the past as well as the present," he told her softly, "and you, fair lady, are taking command of both."

"Oh, don't start that 'fair lady' stuff again." But her voice was airy and her knees weak. She couldn't look away from him.

"You're the kind of woman who inspired knights to great deeds."

"Stop it." She tried to pull away from his hands.

"Agnes." He said her name with gruff rebuke, pulled her toward him swiftly, and put his arms around her. Then with an ease that gave her no time to think he lifted her so she leaned on tiptoe against his chest and clutched his arms for support. Then he kissed her, not forcing it, not having to, because she sighed with defeat and kissed him back.

Aggie delved into his mouth and was rewarded with his swift, hungry response. He was as hard and straight as a fence post against her belly, and his hands tightened on her rib cage then drew upward, lifting her higher. His palms squeezed the sides of her breasts, tantalizing her by not moving closer.

She tried to be neutral with her hands and body, keeping still, shivering with the fear that she was falling into a relationship more powerful than anything she'd ever known before, an affair that was already doomed.

He backed her up to one of the smooth, round porch supports. The wood pressed between her shoulder blades like his accomplice. His hands slid down her hips, cupped under them, and lifted her. Slowly he pressed himself between her legs. She looked at him in a daze of sensation, her hands clenching his sweaty T-shirt at the shoulders but not pushing him away.

His face was ruddy with desire and his mouth looked harsh and tight with restraint. But his eyes reassured her with their gentleness, the incredible patience she'd never seen in a man's passion before.

"Agnes, stop worrying," he whispered. "You always have the power to end this. At any moment it becomes wrong for you."

She nodded woodenly. "It's not wrong to enjoy this." Her voice was barely audible, but filled with the distress she felt. "But it's wrong to take it too much further."

"Only a little further," he promised. Pressing closer, he dropped kisses on her upturned face. She hugged her thighs around his hips. The loose legs of her shorts let his hands slide up until his fingertips were on the soft pads of her buttocks. He held her carefully and flexed into the center of her tender ache. "We're special together," John whispered in the brief moment before his mouth settled on hers again.

Lost in pleasure, Agnes could barely think. What harm would it do to continue this? Her bedroom was so close. She could picture the two of them naked on the white sheets and hear the wicker bedstead creaking with their rhythm. Every feminine need cried out to have his hardness inside her. Her instincts told her he'd probably be as loving as he was lusty, that he wouldn't break this spell.

This spell. She'd lost her common sense. She never wanted to be reckless again. "John, I have to stop," she said softly.

He set her down inch by inch, kissing her face and hair as he did. If he was disappointed or upset there wasn't any sign. He sighed deeply, but it was a happy sound. "That was fantastic, Agnes."

She studied him anxiously. "When I was growing up,

I knew it was okay to kiss and have a little fun then stop. But the rules are different for adults. Kissing means full steam ahead, and nobody's supposed to set limits once the train gets rolling." Hesitating, she added flatly, "My train is happier running by the old rules."

"Agnes," he said as a wry smile curled one corner of his mouth, "you have a train fetish." They both chuckled. She leaned her forehead against his jaw. He stroked her hair. "It's perfectly fine for this train to move slowly."

She curled her fingers into his shirt, liking the friendly feel of soft material and hard muscle beneath it. "I owe you an explanation." She cleared her throat anxiously. "I haven't slept with anyone since I left my husband. More than five years ago."

He was silent for a moment. His hands paused on her hair. Then he said lightly, "Agnes, your train ran off the tracks."

Hearing the humor in his voice made her relax. "I was afraid you'd think I'm weird."

"No. But I'm sure your wheels are rusty."

She choked on laughter. "They are."

He stepped back and looked down at her with gleaming eyes. "No need to justify your good taste."

"Good taste?"

"You waited for me all this time."

He was so glib, she began laughing again. Slowly his fingertips touched her neck, then trailed down to the edge of her T-shirt. She gave a low sigh when he began stroking her breasts with the backs of his fingers. He was barely touching her, his fingers still, only his hands moving, so that the pressure was soft but thick. "Have a good night at your job, Agnes."

He rubbed his fingers over the tips of her breasts, and the bra's sturdy shield of fabric didn't stop sensation from radiating through her. Because he'd reduced her to weak-kneed silence, she merely nodded.

"I'll find my way through the woods to your camp-ground," he continued.

"Hmmm."

"And set up my tent. I'll introduce myself to any nervous senior citizens and assure them I'm a friend of the owner's."

"The Cranshaws. Here for the whole summer. In charge."

"What time should I stop by tomorrow?"

"Noon."

"Very good. I had a wonderful day today, Agnes. Thank you for the bandage on my thumb. I'll treasure it." He raised his softly swathed thumb to her chin, caressing her. She lifted her mouth to his one more time. When she looked into his eyes, they were amused and admiring. "Good evening," he whispered.

"Evening."

He moved away, went down the porch steps, and walked to his Jeep. Leaning on the porch post, Aggie watched him, feeling drained but greedy. Her mind was blank. He smiled at her as he started the Jeep, then put his fingertips to his lips for a moment as he drove out of the yard.

She slid down the porch post and sat on the steps, her hands limp in her lap. She was already half in love with John Bartholomew, and she'd only known him one day.

Her house was filled with small things that defined her. In the narrow beam of John's flashlight they appeared in the darkness like still lifes from a slide show, illuminated brightly for a second, then lost again. Hanging from the back of the living-room door was an orange canvas tote bag with a bright African design. Stuffed in the bottom were the year's receipts for horse feed and veterinary service, all stamped 'Paid.' Her record system struck him as creative but reckless.

Faded but sturdy old furniture filled the living room, and the walls were covered in flowered paper and framed photographs of quarter horses and ornate ribbons from breeders' shows, many of them dating back twenty years. There were photos of her grandfather, Sam Hamilton, a redheaded, pug-nosed old man with a lined face, beaming at a prize horse in one picture; in another photo he was an earnest-looking younger man in an army uniform with captain's insignia.

John looked at the photo with disgust. Here was Captain Samuel Hamilton, the thief who had stolen valuable heirlooms from a helpless English family during the war. This man had doomed John's maternal grandparents and through them, his mother. But not him, not after he got the books back.

John swung the flashlight's beam away. Agnes wouldn't be home from her job for hours—what was he hesitating for?

Those manuscripts might be here, somewhere, and he hoped to find a clue.

He slipped down the back hall off the living room, his well-worn jogging shoes making very little noise on the old wood floor. The flashlight lit a large room with a four-poster brass bed and straight plaid curtains. One glance at the room's masculine decor told John it had belonged to Aggie's grandfather.

The room next to it was an office. Shelves lined the whitewashed walls, filled with show trophies, framed pictures, and books of all kinds. Under them in one corner was a rolltop desk scattered with unpaid bills and a chipped ceramic vase crowned with a dusty silk begonia. John scanned the books, noticing all the volumes on Latin and medieval history.

His heart pounded. He dropped his attention to books stacked on the desk. Tucked among them was a notepad. The writing was bold and feminine. Agnes's.

He removed the notepad and studied it, reading

exactly what he'd hoped to find, notes about twelfth-century English history, knights, the Tower of London, and King Henry II.

The period was right. The details were perfect. John had no doubt that her grandfather had left her the medieval diary and prayer book. He hoped they were hidden in this room.

A night breeze suddenly cascaded through the sheer white curtains. John shut off his flashlight and straightened warily in the darkness, watching the luminous material billow. Goosebumps ran up his spine. He didn't believe in omens, but shame washed over him.

He was so dishonorable sneaking around Agnes's home this way! It was beneath him, beneath his code of—of what? Chivalry? He was no fantasy figure, except when he tried to charm Agnes.

John slapped the flashlight hard against his palm. He deserved those books! He didn't give a tinker's damn about the contents or the sentimental value, and he wouldn't let them take over his imagination this way!

*This is beneath my honor,* a stubborn inner voice insisted.

The thought stayed as though he'd stored it in some quiet alcove long ago. It had only been waiting for the right moment to slip free.

John slammed his hand against the desk. The vase bounced and made a rattling sound. Gritting his teeth, he quickly shoved the notepad back where it had been. He was careful not to leave anything out of place. In his career with Scotland Yard he'd been meticulous about details. Sorrow twisted his stomach as he recalled how proud he'd been of his work—and how good he'd been at it.

He strode out of the office and paused in the hallway, looking toward the back of the house. He wanted to see Agnes's bedroom for reasons having nothing to do with finding the books.

It was across the hall, a small, neat room with a wicker bedstead painted white and covered in bright-white linens, with no quilt or blanket. The double bed sat among plain wooden furniture and braided throw rugs. Bottles of perfume and cosmetics were arranged on a dresser beside a stuffed alligator.

Gingham curtains rippled seductively at a large window near the head of the bed. A large bookcase contained a stereo and tape deck, a small portable television, a collection of quartz crystals, seashells, ordinary-looking rocks, and pine cones.

With a sense of wonder he touched the whimsical collection, the funny little alligator, the crisp white bed sheets. No matter how ugly her past was, it didn't cling to her the way his clung to him. Her room was serene and wholesome, an ice-cream-parlor sort of place but filled with the provocative presence of a mature woman. The perfumes were spicy and exotic, and among her makeup selection was a tube of scorching red lipstick.

He liked her contradictions. He wanted to believe that if she knew why he'd come here she'd turn over the books with an innocent apology for her grandfather's crime. And then what?

John stood in the center of her room, squinting thoughtfully into space. Then he'd sell the books for the fortune they'd bring, buy Agnes wonderful gifts and whisk her off to someplace luxurious, where the two of them could concentrate on becoming lovers.

Unless she hated him for the lies he'd let her believe so far.

Abruptly he headed back to the front of the house. Agnes would understand. He'd explain. He wouldn't let doubts close in on him.

He'd gotten inside her front door easily, jimmying the lock. He relocked the door and absentmindedly patted Agnes's dogs, who crowded around his legs. His affection for animals was as natural as the instinct to breathe. Tonight he'd have to yell at the friendly mutts or they'd follow him back to the campground.

But as he crossed the yard they began barking and ran toward the barn. He followed them behind it to the pasture fence. There, near the gate to the corral, stood one of the mares by herself. She had her head down and was sniffing the ground, while her hooves shifted restlessly.

John went to her, crooning under his breath. He examined her and stroked her distended stomach. "Looks as though you're about to drop a bun from that oven." Her ears twitched. She seemed to appreciate the coarse slang and the bawdy accent in his voice.

He slapped her rump. "Haul your muffins to the maternity ward." Taking her by the forelock, he led her into the barn. Here was a way to make up to Agnes for roaming about her house uninvited. He'd play midwife.

Aggie was frightened when she drove into her yard at two-thirty in the morning and found the barn lights blazing. Her dogs nearly tripped her with their welcome, licking her white jeans legs, stepping on her white sneakers, and bouncing up to nip at the hem of the flowered shirt she wore over a pink tank top. They weren't nervous, she thought, and they would be if a stranger were in the barn.

She stopped cautiously in the barn's hall, seeing nothing above the stalls' head-high partitions. "Who's here?"

No answer. Only a stall door at the hall's far end was shut. She strode to it, her heart hammering in her chest, and peered over the door. A long, slow sigh of tenderness and amazement slipped from her throat. Curled up on a fresh bed of wood shavings was her bay mare, Dottie.

Dottie's eyelashes fluttered as her head nodded drowsily. John was asleep beside her, looking grimy, disheveled, but very appealing in rumpled old trousers and no shirt. His head rested on Dottie's plump shoulder.

And stretched out beside him, snoring, with its tiny bay head on his bare stomach, was Dottie's newborn foal. John had draped one arm around its neck. The foal's stubby black tail twitched with contentment.

Aggie propped her arms on the door and rested her chin on them. She knew she had a giddy smile on her face as she studied the scene in front of her.

John Bartholomew was wonderful.

# *Five*

She hoped he liked oatmeal. Bustling around her small, bright kitchen, Aggie dropped utensils, bumped into the old Formica-topped table, and nearly stirred sugar instead of salt into the bubbling pot on the stove. Her attention was distracted by listening for any sound of John moving around in her grandfather's room, where he'd spent what was left of the night after they stopped baby-sitting the new foal.

As she began quartering oranges on a cutting board by the sink, she heard his footsteps on the bedroom floor and almost poked her finger with the paring knife. Exasperated, she leaned close to the open window over the sink, pulled the tail of her floppy blue tank top out of her cutoffs, and fanned herself.

The creak of the bedroom door made her tuck the top into her shorts hurriedly and smooth the fine curly tendrils escaping from her hair, which she'd braided loosely down her back. She didn't want to look like a woman who wanted to impress a man—but she was.

His long, solid strides on the hall's wooden floor made her hands tremble. She grabbed a piece of orange and fiddled with the peel as if removing it were an art that required concentration.

"You're a very pleasant sight to see first thing in the morning," John said from the doorway.

She smiled over her shoulder and kept working. "Hi. Hope you like hot mushy food."

"Hmmm." He went to the stove and lifted the lid on the oatmeal. "Gruel. My favorite."

Aggie glanced toward him, trying not to stare happily. His ruffled hair and sleepy expression were very sensual. He wore loose white trousers and a white tank top similar to her own—except that it was tight and what it revealed of his hard, darkly haired chest was more interesting than looking at herself. His expression as he sniffed the pot of oatmeal made her burst into laughter. "Don't call my oatmeal 'gruel.'"

His attention flickered down her body for a moment, but politely. She was as soft and hot inside as the oatmeal by the time he met her gaze again. "Good morning."

She managed a jaunty nod. "Morning."

"I didn't mean to sleep late."

"You didn't. It's only seven."

"I didn't want to miss anything."

"I only got up thirty minutes ago. I checked on Dottie and the little guy. They're fine."

"He's got the look of a winner to me."

"I hope some buyer agrees with you in about ten months."

"You won't consider keeping him?"

She shook her head, feeling a surge of regret. "I've got no time to train and show weanlings, even the best ones. I'd like to show my own horses someday, but I can't right now."

"You need a partner."

Her hands fumbled with the orange slice. *A prosperous English businessman, maybe?* But she'd never bring that subject up with him. She had too much pride. And she was cautious where her ranch was concerned. It was all she had.

Was it smart to be cautious about the ranch but reckless about falling in love with him? Aggie frowned at the irony.

"You're thinking about something awfully hard, Agnes," he said lightly. "I can almost see a vein throbbing in your forehead."

"Aw, that's just the soft spot."

He reached out and touched his fingertips to the bruise near her hairline. "Feeling better?"

"Yeah. How about you?" She lifted his left hand and examined the bruised thumb.

"First rate. I like comparing injuries with you. We have a lot in common."

"Bruises don't count." She released his hand and looked at him wistfully. "They heal, and you forget about them."

"Don't be practical, Agnes. Perhaps I wasn't talking about heads and thumbs."

"Oh? Well, I wish all my problems got better so fast."

"Tell me your problems. I'll be the doctor."

She grinned. "Oh, no, I'm not ready to play doctor with you."

"Don't I look professional?" He waved a hand at his white trousers and tank top.

"You look like the lead in an Italian art film. All you need is a scarf around your neck and a cigarette hanging out of your mouth. Come on, gimme a sultry look and say *ciao*."

He gave her a slit-eyed smile. "*Ciao, seducente.*"

The look wasn't just sultry, it had a knowing, predatory edge that seemed to belong to some other man, a less lighthearted one. Feeling nervous, she turned her attention back to the overworked orange. "No fair ad-libbing."

"Agnes?" he said, sounding concerned. "*Seducente* means 'gorgeous.' It's a compliment."

"Oh, I know. When I was living in California I had an Italian housekeeper. She taught me a few naughty words to impress my, uh, husband." She winced inwardly and thought, *Smart, Hamilton*. John had complimented her, and in reply she'd brought up her intimacy with another man.

John leaned, hip-shot, against the countertop and propped a hand on the old blue tiles. "Ah-hah. So he was obviously *seducente*. The lady reveals a bit of her carefully guarded history. Tell me more." His casual stance was as deceptive as her relaxed smile. She saw the glitter of intense emotion in his eyes and the hardness in his mouth.

"Tell me about all the women you've loved," she countered, still smiling.

"Loved? That narrows the field. Love is when you dote on the idea of sharing another person's life, warts and all, for every day of the rest of *your* life. I've been infatuated with a person here and there, but I've never loved anyone, by my definition of the word."

"You and your definitions," she said dryly. "I'd like to have a copy of the dictionary you use."

He laughed but bowed his head to her with a gallantry that made her catch her breath. "It's all stored in my heart."

"Must be crowded, your heart. Wouldn't want you to clog a valve."

"Agnes, the heart is as big as a person's spirit." His voice dropped to a teasing, seductive level. "And as eternal as a person's true desires."

Her hands trembled. She couldn't let her imagination get the best of her. "I'll tell you what eternity is," she replied lightly. "It's waiting for oatmeal to finish cooking when you're hungry."

"Whatever you say, Agnes."

She picked up her paring knife and jabbed an orange with it. "Don't sound smug."

"I'm glad I'm not an orange."

Aggie pointed the impaled fruit toward a percolator plugged into an electrical outlet above the countertop. "You're in luck. I calm down after I have my morning cup of coffee. Grab those two mugs and pour us some. We've got things to do."

"Such as?"

"Go to the beach. I owe you some fun for all you did yesterday." *Not to mention the wonderful things you did to me on the porch*, she added silently.

"You don't owe me, Agnes," he said, frowning.

"I want to, okay?" They were silent, sharing a quiet look. He searched her eyes and she stood still, mesmerized. Slowly he smiled. "I'd love it, then. Very much."


John told himself he was building character. Yes, if he could lie on the warm sand next to Agnes without putting a hand on her, he had more character than he'd ever guessed he had.

"Spring is the perfect time of year to be here," she told him. "The weather's still a little cool." She chuckled. "Eighty-five degrees instead of ninety-five." Her fair complexion was tinted a warm pink by the sunlight filtering through the enormous red beach umbrella they'd rented. They lay on their stomachs on a colorful blanket, chins propped on their arms. "And on a weekday morning like this, there isn't much of a crowd."

"It's wonderful." John gazed at her as he said that. "Not crowded at all."

Her lips pursed in a mild taunt. "Not where you're looking."

"You're looking back."

"I like the scenery."

"Hmmm. I like your honesty."

She fluttered her lashes at him. "I'm looking at the dunes behind you. The sea oats are so pretty."

"Then you must have incredible side vision, because those eccentric blue eyes haven't strayed from my handsome self one bit."

"Eccentric eyes? What a description! You want me to drop a jellyfish on your back?"

"They're odd in a lovely way, Agnes. They fade inward, as if you'd splashed silver paint into a bucket of blue."

"You're getting poetic on me. I'll blush."

"We'll make each other blush."

"This is a public beach."

He grinned at her, silently cursed the fact that it was a public beach, and turned his face forward before he was tempted to kiss her. He was aching for much more than a kiss. The soft sand was a welcome cushion for his arousal.

John focused his attention on the panorama of wide white beach and blue-green ocean. A few couples strolled near the tide line, and children squatted in the surf picking up shells. It was peaceful scenery, he thought, and ought to soothe him.

But he shut his eyes and pictured the ocean breeze stroking a loose strand of Agnes's hair, the umbrella's fringe making little shadows across the bridge of her tilted nose, highlighting the scattered freckles there. He smelled her suntan lotion and thought how good her oiled skin would feel under his hands.

"Where in the world did you get that old-fashioned swimsuit?" he asked abruptly. He rolled over on his back and latched his hands under his head, then stared casually up at the umbrella. Her two-piece suit was bright red too.

She chuckled. "A rummage sale. It must have been made back in the fifties. It was faded, so I dyed it. Otherwise, it's good as new."

She rolled onto her back, too, then tucked a towel

under her head as a pillow. John allowed himself a glance at the swimsuit's bottom piece. It covered her flat belly and full hips in snug red pleats. The suit might as well have been one-piece.

It hid her from thighs to waist and let only a narrow band of skin show between the bottom and top pieces. The top was similarly pleated and modest, anchoring her full, ripe breasts with its wide shoulder bands and sturdy gathers in the center.

But no matter how modest the swimsuit was, Agnes filled it with the kind of bounce and sway that gave men eye strain. "I like it," he told her. "But what made you choose an old style?"

"I got tired of bikinis. Every time I went in the ocean all I did was hold the top half down and the bottom half up. I nearly drowned once, trying to keep my dignity."

He would have paid for the privilege of rescuing her from *that* predicament. "Why not buy a one-piece, then?"

"Too see-through for my taste. Last one I owned was so sheer when it got wet I swore I could see my tattoos through it."

Smiling at her nonsense, he turned on his side and rose on an elbow. "Tattoos? Really? Where?" She'd given him a perfect excuse to study her. He scanned her torso with solemn innocence.

She laughed. "No tattoos. But if I'd had some, you could have seen them. So I bought this little red dinosaur, and it works just fine. It's a nineteen-fifties suit, and I've got a nineteen-fifties body. Lots of padding and no sharp angles. I'm a throwback."

"You're perfect." He gestured from her neck to her thighs, skimming his fingertips just above her body. "This sort of body made Marilyn Monroe a star."

"Wow. Paint-bucket eyes and Marilyn's body. I could learn to like your brand of flattery."

"I'm being honest with you." John leaned over. Her

nostrils flared a little, and her eyes widened. She lay as still as the sand, watching him. "You're very beautiful. Please don't think I'm flirting." He hesitated, his mouth twitching with humor. "It *is* flirting but it's sincere."

She dampened her lips with the tip of her tongue. "I've never heard of anybody around here getting in trouble for kissing on a public beach."

He put a hand on the center of her stomach. The small patch of bare skin, such an innocent part of a woman's body, was a silky table making him anxious to explore more of it. She trembled under his fingertips.

"We're very secluded, back here by the dunes," he agreed, sliding his propped arm next to her head so he could lower his head close to hers. "No one's paying any attention to us."

"Would you mind if we didn't do anything except kiss?" Her eyes flickered with uncertainty, despite her droll expression. "I don't feel like Marilyn Monroe in this bathing suit, I feel like Doris Day. And Doris never did anything but kiss."

The hot breeze lifted a strand of red hair across her face. He drew the hair aside, letting the pad of his thumb trace her cheek. "I don't want to hurt the friendship we have. And there's no hurry."

"John Bartholomew." She said only his name, but put a world of meaning into it, tentative affection and desire, as if she were testing her emotions out loud, to see what would happen. She touched his lips with her fingers, traced his mouth, then slid her hand in one smooth caress along his cheek until finally her fingers speared into his hair.

"Don't ever change," she whispered. "You're the sweetest man I've ever met. You really do have an aura of goodness around you."

Her words tormented him. He wasn't good, but she was. There was a helluva lot more to her than he'd learned when he'd researched her past. He sensed that just like him, she'd been hurt badly by the people in her life. She was desperate to trust somebody, and she wanted to trust him.

And he wanted to deserve that trust.

"You're thinking too hard," she teased gently.

"Trying to decide which corner of your mouth to kiss first. You have sexy lips, Agnes. I can't tell which lip is nicer. I think it's a tie."

She grinned. "Kiss me, and I'll help you decide."

When he lowered his mouth onto hers she mewled softly and opened her lips, at first playful as she kissed him, then so intense it was all he could do to keep from snatching her into his arms. John shuddered with delight. A sudden and vivid rush of emotion made him feel like a teenager again. Because kissing was the only intimacy he and she could share, restraint heightened every erotic sensation.

He could hardly keep his hand still on her stomach, and underneath it her body flexed like the swells of the ocean. He pictured her giving in to that strong force. He pictured himself riding her currents.

When she moaned into his mouth and he shuddered in response he knew it was time to stop, before he gave in to an urge to seduce her. He already wanted to lead her deep into the sand dunes, where no one could see what they did next.

He couldn't let himself do that. When they were naked and he was making love to her with wild abandon she might doubt his gentlemanly talk about being patient, to say the least. He wanted her to trust him, not wonder if he were manipulating her.

Quickly John pulled back. Looking down into her half shut eyes and flushed face, with its charged expression of desire, he was amazed at his self-control. Maybe there was a little of Sir Miles's chivalry in his blood, after all. "You've been alone a long time," he whispered, "and I don't want to take advantage of that, Agnes."

She frowned and raised a shaking hand to her forehead, as if trying to remember where she was. "No, I don't want to be careless. I know better than to move too fast." Her lips were damp and dark red from the pressure of his mouth. John stared at them in fascination, aching to kiss her again. "Kissing each other is not such an innocent thing, after all," he admitted.

"Not the way you do it." She looked regretful. "I've been alone because I wanted it that way. But maybe it's time I took some risks again."

John brushed his lips over hers. Her low sigh of pleasure and the flavor of her mouth nearly made him forget his troubled thoughts. "You taste like those orange slices from breakfast." He caught her lower lip in a quick sucking motion then released it. "What a meal I could make of you, my lady."

Her tiny moan of delight made him kiss her again, and their tongues met in a slow, devastating dance inside her mouth. But she began patting his shoulder almost frantically. He knew what she meant and forced himself to move back.

Sitting up, he faced the ocean and propped his arms on updrawn knees. He took deep breaths of ocean breeze and concentrated on the squawking white gulls constantly patrolling the beach. She sat up also, hugged her knees, and stared silently toward a distant horizon where tiny ships crossed the line between ocean and sky.

John still felt as if she were kissing him. It wasn't only the desire crackling between them like tendrils of static; it was knowing they had something special, a closeness hinting at shared dreams and shared problems.

"Agnes, there are a thousand subjects I want to discuss with you," he said slowly, still looking straight ahead so he wouldn't break down and kiss her again. "Everything from your favorite flavor of ice cream to your lifelong ambitions and deepest fears. Everything you want, or love, or hate. But right now there's one thing I have to ask."

"I don't think I'm going to like it," she warned softly. She ran a hand through her hair wearily, tearing at a snarl in the red strands. "But go ahead."

He twisted a little so he could watch her expression. "Only a man you cared enough about to marry could turn you into such a loner. What did your husband do to you?"

A shuttered look came over her face, and her eyes filled with doubt as they searched his. John cupped the side of her face and made a soothing sound low in his throat. "I'm not going to judge you by anyone else's faults. If I were that kind of bastard, I'd have turned away from you when Mrs. Roberts made her stupid little remarks about you. But I'm not a narrow-minded fool."

Tears rose in her eyes. "I guess you wouldn't settle for learning my favorite flavor of ice cream? It's vanilla. Vanilla's simple, classic, and it doesn't surprise you. No matter how it's made, vanilla's always about the same."

"*Agnes,*" he said sternly.

She sighed and faced the ocean again. "It's true about him being a drug dealer. Big-time. Upper-management level," she added bitterly. "Never got his hands or his respectable image dirty."

"When did you find out?"

"Not long before he was arrested. We'd been married for about three years."

"He didn't use drugs himself?"

"At parties, sometimes." She hesitated, a muscle popping in her jaw, then added, "So did I."

"Were you addicted?"

"No, nothing that awful. I wanted to fit in. It wasn't cool to say no. And to be honest, I was so depressed about who I was that I wanted something to make me feel better."

He put a hand on the back of her neck and massaged

the sinew that made a thick ridge there. "Who were you, then?"

"An ex-child star nobody recognized anymore. A bargain-basement actress who wasn't trained to be anything else. I'd worked in the business since I was a *baby*, for godsakes. When I couldn't get jobs anymore, I felt lost and worthless. I tried going to college, but I couldn't hack the routine."

"You're a smart, disciplined person. I can't believe you dropped out of college simply because it was difficult."

"But see, I didn't know how to adjust to classrooms and strict schedules and all those things. I never went to high school!"

"You can't mean you never got an education."

"No, I have a high school diploma. But I never had a high school. Tutors were hired to teach me while I worked. On breaks during the day. That was the only time I had for school. By comparison, college was too slow for me. Boring."

"I can't picture you failing at college because of laziness."

"Okay, okay, there were a lot of reasons. But I could have tried harder."

"What held you back?"

"I spent too much time running after Richard, doing whatever he wanted. He didn't like me being preoccupied with college. He never saw the point in getting more education when you already have money. He complained so much about my schedule, I quit."

"Richard, eh? I'm glad to know his name. Now he isn't an anonymous face in my mind. I can picture him."

"Oh? What do you think he looks like?"

"He has fangs, pasty skin, and he turns into a bat each night."

She gave a short laugh. "If nothing else, you described his personality."

"Tell me more about this vampire."

"He owned a real-estate company. Sold expensive houses to expensive people. He was about ten years older than I and *very* sophisticated. He wore designer suits, spent money like there was no tomorrow, and made me feel important even though I wasn't a TV star anymore."

"I suspect you needed him for the wrong reasons, reasons you didn't understand until you were older."

"No, I can't blame my mistakes on being too young. I was twenty-two when I married him, but the way I grew up, that wasn't young. I spent my whole childhood working as a professional actor. I was expected to be a pint-sized adult. I grew up too fast."

"Precisely. You never had a normal life. You were inexperienced, in that sense."

"'Inexperienced' sounds better than 'confused and stupid,' which was what I was."

"Sssh. If Richard made it impossible for you to go to college, what did he expect you to be?"

"A lot of fun," she answered grimly. "His own private party girl." She roughly brushed sand off her toes. "I was good at it, too."

"What happened after he was arrested?"

"The government seized everything he owned, which meant everything I owned, since it was all in Richard's name. He went to prison. He's still there."

"And you were left with nothing?"

"Yep. One week I was living in a Malibu beach house and shopping in Beverly Hills, the next I was selling my wedding ring to buy groceries and rent a cheap apartment."

"That was when you moved here to live with your grandfather?"

She laughed ruefully. "No, I wasn't gonna go down without a fight. I stayed in California for about another year. I wanted to prove the tabloid stories were wrong. I wasn't just another washed-up kiddie star who'd made some stupid mistakes."

She swiped a finger across her mouth as if there were a bad taste there. "Then I made some more mistakes. Nothing I want to talk about."

She didn't have to. John knew what she meant. He'd seen a tape of the TV movie she'd made. Agnes had portrayed a young cocktail waitress who seduced and then blackmailed all the ministers in a small Midwestern town. The plot was no more than an excuse for scene after scene of smirking sexual innuendo.

The movie had been badly written and poorly made. And Agnes, as she'd already admitted to him, was a mediocre actress. Her primary purpose in the film had been to wander around in a breathtaking variety of lingerie.

When he'd watched the tape, John had laughed at her acting ability and made bawdy, admiring comments about her body. Now he felt a deep stab of sympathy for her and an urge to strangle the filmmakers who'd humiliated her in that piece of trash.

John turned his hand palm up along her neck and began drawing his fingers through her thick hair, carefully untangling the curls and smoothing them. "Let's keep talking about Richard. Do you still love him a little?"

"I never loved Richard," she retorted so quickly that she almost spat the words. "I had love confused with need. I needed emotional security. I thought having a husband would give me that. Now I know I'm my own security, and the only thing I need a husband for is . . . nothing. I don't need a husband at all, come to think of it."

John frowned at her. "Don't let Richard turn you off about love and marriage forever. There's nothing more wonderful than a loving partnership between a man and a woman." The moment he finished saying those words, he was astonished. He almost believed them. This was carrying things a little too far.

She grasped one of his shoulders and looked him in the eye with steely dismay. "You're a doll, and when you leave I'll miss you. I'm already sure of that. But you come from some kind of fairy-tale world. You wouldn't recognize real life from a hole in the ground."

"I haven't lived in the clouds, Agnes. I know what the real world's like."

"Right. A place where rich little boys go to private schools and rich young men go to Oxford, before they inherit the family business and become rich young men who have so much money they can take a month off to hang out in America."

John told himself to ignore the anger rising in his chest. If she knew the harsh truth about his background she wouldn't be so smug. "I don't get the feeling you grew up poor or downtrodden, Agnes. You certainly didn't marry a poor man, from what you've told me."

She went very still, looking stunned and then furious. "I made my parents rich," she said slowly, between gritted teeth. "But we lived one step ahead of the creditors. That Ferrari I told you about? It was repossessed, just like every car we ever owned. My parents never held on to a dollar long enough to make the paper warm."

"Richard must have looked like a security blanket. No wonder you thought you loved him."

Her face turned white. She got to her knees. "Are you askin' me if I married him for his money?"

"Did you?"

His candid question apparently shocked her. "Maybe I did!" she blurted out. "Maybe I loved his money as much as I loved him. Don't look at me that way. Don't you dare."

"You're seeing what your defensiveness expects to see, not what I feel. Don't overreact."

"You're judging me!"

"You're judging yourself. Calm down."

"I don't need your do-goodin' attitude, okay? I don't want your pity either."

John ground his teeth. His sympathy was fading. She was taking advantage of the courtesy she claimed to adore, knocking him for not being cynical enough. He had plenty of cynicism, if she wanted to know the truth. In a tight, controlled voice he said, "Agnes, I think you'd like to be a bully."

"No, I just have a fine-tuned ear for hypocrisy. Guess it comes from being misjudged too often by strangers."

"You're accusing an innocent man."

"No wonder you love all that medieval hogwash about chivalry. You're a real Sir Galahad, I admit it, but maybe that's because you can afford to be. Get real."

John seethed inside. He'd busted his bum trying to make her happy with some bloody silly fantasy about him, restrained himself from taking advantage of her loneliness, listened to her sorrows with a kind ear, and all it had gotten him were accusations. He'd been wrongly accused too damned much in the past year.

John grabbed one of her hands, kissed it roughly, then set it back in her lap. "You're a snob, Agnes. I feel sorry for you."

"Sorry for me?" she repeated, her voice rising. "I never asked for your sympathy!"

"You need a great deal more than my sympathy. You need for me to shake up your lopsided notions about how men and women are supposed to act. For one thing, when a man treats you nicely, you shouldn't yell at him like a shrew."

"This isn't a medieval fairy-tale! This is real life! When it comes down to the nitty-gritty, don't expect me to play Lady Agnes for you!"

# YOU GET SIX ROMANCES RISK FREE...
# *Plus* AN EXCLUSIVE TITLE FREE!

## *Loveswept Romances*

:::::::::::::::::::::::::::::::::::::

AFFIX
RISK FREE
BOOKS
STAMP
HERE.

:::::::::::::::::::::::::::::::::::::

Kay Hooper's
**Larger Than Life**

This FREE gift
is yours to keep.

## MY "NO RISK" GUARANTEE

There's no obligation to buy and the free gift is mine to keep. I may preview each subsequent shipment for 15 days. If I don't want it, I simply return the books within 15 days and owe nothing. If I keep them, I will pay just $2.25 per book. I save $3.00 off the retail price for the 6 books (plus postage and handling, and sales tax in NY).

**YES!** Please send my six Loveswept novels RISK FREE along with my FREE GIFT described inside the heart! **BR90**    41228

NAME_____

ADDRESS_____APT_____

CITY_____

STATE_____ZIP_____

"Would you trust me more if I'd taken advantage of your hungry little body a few minutes ago? I could have, and you know it. But I didn't. Make up your mind—am I a hero or a fool for treating you with respect?"

"You're not either! You're just a different type of man, one I haven't figured out yet!"

"This conversation is pointless. Let's change clothes and go to one of the restaurants along the beach. We'll have an early lunch. You could use a soothing cup of clam chowder. Heavy on the clams."

"I think I'd better drop you off at the campground. Then you can do what you want, and I'll go to my interview."

"Oh, no. You're not going to back out on your invitation. I'm going with you to see that model-train craftsman."

"He's not a *craftsman*, he's a weird little old man nicknamed Squid, who builds miniature tanker cars out of salt shakers and trees out of broccoli covered in shellac! My world isn't classy, John! You don't know much about me or my life, but you think you have all the answers. You don't!"

He stood and held out a hand. He'd had enough. "Get up, Agnes, and stop caterwauling. I'm sorry the subject of your ex-husband upsets you. But don't transfer your anger to me."

"*Caterwauling?*" she echoed, crouching on all fours. "You self-satisfied horse's ass."

"You need a bit of cooling off, my lady." He snagged her under both arms, pulled her to her feet, then in the same motion threw her over one shoulder. He pivoted and carried her toward the surf.

She had too much pride to squeal in public. So she hung there, her short-nailed fingers digging into his lower back, while she hissed in a whisper, "Stop! Set me down!" Several children playing nearby screamed with laughter and called to their parents to watch.

"Agnes, I'm going to tell you something, and I want you never to forget it." John plowed into the surf until the water reached his waist. He dumped her sideways into the swirling waves. When she clambered to her feet, slinging her hair back and balling her fists, he pointed a finger at her calmly. "I'm not Richard."

She halted, her lips parting in a silent O of shock. Then the fight drained out of her, and her fists sank into the water, unfurling. "I know that."

"You know it, but you don't believe it. You'll go on treating me as a threat until you accept the fact that not all men are like him. Accept me for what I am, and don't hate me unless I give you reason to."

"I don't hate you. Why do you think I was kissing you a minute ago?"

"Oh, but kissing is such an easy thing to do."

"It's the *best* I can do right now!"

"That's fine, but I want an apology for those terrible things you said to me."

"I only meant you shouldn't give me advice on love and marriage. You've never been married! You've never really been in love!"

"But I know what I want." He held out his hands. What he said next was a shock to them both. "I want to marry you, Agnes."

She froze, staring at him as if he were crazy. Then a look of understanding dawned on her face, and she burst into laughter. "You sure know how to change the mood," she said between chortles, swaying as if the sheer absurdity of his proposal made her weak. "That's the best thing you could have said. All right, truce! You and me get married—agggh!" She shook her head and bent over, laughing harder.

John stared at her in dismay. He didn't know why he'd proposed. He'd had a feeling all along that things were going to explode in some unpredictable way be-

tween him and Agnes, some way neither of them could
imagine yet. This was proof of it. But he knew one thing
right now, as he examined his bruised emotions.

She thought he was kidding.

To his amazement, he wasn't.

# Six

On a Saturday night in the height of the spring tourist season the Conquistador Pub was so crowded with tourists it threatened to fall off its weathered gray pilings into the bay. The Jimmy Buffet imitator working the tiny corner stage had his amplifier turned up louder than usual, and a delivery boy handed Aggie a flowering cactus. She halted in the middle of her busy chores and lost all her concentration.

*Prickly*, the accompanying note said. *But lovely when it blooms.*

Aggie shoved the cactus into a back corner of the bar, crumpled the notecard and poked it into the red-clay pot, then stood staring blankly at the plant, a grin on her face.

"Whozit from?" growled the bar's owner, a middle-aged man with crew-cut gray hair, a Navy insignia tattooed on one beefy bicep, and a big, sweet heart under his attitude. Retired Chief Petty Officer Oscar Rattinelli, "Rat" to those willing to risk a broken face, peered over her shoulder as he waited for a blender to finish churning up a Pink Rum Punch.

"Guy named John Bartholomew." Aggie flipped a beer glass under the tap on the wall next to John's gift cactus. "Been staying at my campground for the past week."

"Decent?"

"Too decent."

"Why?"

"Asked me to marry him."

Oscar nearly dropped the blender. "He *what*?"

"He asked me to marry him. One week ago, he asked me."

"What'd you say?"

She handed the frosty mug of beer to a customer at the packed bar, smoothly pivoting around three hundred pounds of stunned Oscar. "I laughed harder than I've laughed in years."

"What'd he say then?"

"Said he wished a seam would pop in my swimsuit."

"How d'ya know he was just kidding about the marriage stuff?"

"He's got class. He was only trying to make a point."

"Whatzat?"

"That he's got class."

"Oh. I'm confused."

"He respects me. That's what."

"Oh. He better. Papa Rattinelli would break all his fingers, if you say the word."

"Nah. But thanks." She patted Oscar's enormous shoulder with her free hand while she poured a shooter of whiskey for another customer.

"I have to take care of you. You're the best bartender I've ever had. And the prettiest. And the only one who didn't quit the first time I yelled at her."

"I yell back."

"That's why you're special. If I had a daughter, I'd want her to yell just like you."

"You're sweeter than key-lime pie for worrying about me. But don't. John is a cross between Prince Charles and a Boy Scout. He helps little old ducks cross the road."

"Whatzis? He's helping out around your lake?"

"Yeah. And the old folks love him as much as the old ducks do. He rebuilt the carburetor on the Cranshaws' Winnebago."

"They're back again for another whole season?"

"Yeah. Just like the past four years. I gave them the same deal they had with Grandpa—free use of a site and utilities in return for supervising the whole campground. They collect fees, keep the place cleaned up, and call me if any of the other guests get rowdy."

"And they like this Bartholomew guy too, huh?"

She nodded vaguely and muttered to herself, "Funny, I wouldn't have thought he'd know how to fix a carburetor. Especially after the model train thing."

"Model train thing?"

"I did an interview with Squid Davis at the toy shop. John went with me. Oscar, if you owned a chain of hobby shops that sold, among other things, model trains, wouldn't you know better than to lay your car keys on Squid's electrified track?"

"I guess. Is that what John did?"

"Yeah. Blew a fuse in Squid's control box. Nearly derailed the whole Gulf and Western freight line."

"And this John guy claims to be a model train expert?"

"Said he only *owns* the shops. He doesn't actually build model trains himself."

"Executive type, huh?"

"Very uppercrust British executive type. But an outdoorsman too."

"So he's spending his whole vacation at your campground?"

"No, he's spending it building a back porch on my house."

"Why?"

"He likes porches."

"What does he do besides build porches?"

"Quotes Greek philosophers. Discusses medieval history. Plays a fine game of Monopoly. Cheats at cards, but he admits it. Cleans barns, charms lady horses."

"Charms lady horses?"

"Yeah. All six of my mares have a crush on him. He's a natural with them. And he's already got my new colt halter broken."

"Sounds like he's got you halter broken too."

Speechless, she considered Oscar's observation. He was probably right. When she wasn't with John all she did was think about him, and every day she became more willing to tag along behind him as docilely as Dottie's new colt. But she wasn't going to admit that to anyone. She playfully flicked a bar towel at Oscar. "Nah. I can't get rid of him, that's all."

"You're smiling again."

Her expression fell. "Yeah. Can't stop," she said grimly. "That's the problem."

"What you gonna do?"

"Take him to a nice restaurant tomorrow night, for one thing. Spend every free minute in the next three weeks with him, for another. Keep smiling till he leaves."

"Where's he going?"

"Home. To Merry Old England."

"Oh. What'll you do then?"

Aggie pulled the cactus forward and stroked its pink blossoms. She angled her face so Oscar wouldn't see how upset she was. "Wake up and stop dreaming."

If any of his old friends in London knew he'd proposed marriage to a woman he'd met little more than a week ago, they'd place bets on his sanity. John wouldn't blame them. While driving through the dusky evening down a pleasant St. Augustine boulevard lined with shops and palm trees he struggled with the question that had bothered him all week.

He'd gone too far with his deception. He hadn't had to propose marriage to win her confidence! He was working steadily toward that goal and making progress every day. Proposing out of the blue to her had been the most bewildering thing he'd done in his whole life. How low would he sink to charm her? It was despicable, asking her to marry him.

But he hadn't been thinking about his motives when he'd asked her. He'd only been thinking that it was the right thing to want.

The hot sun must have gotten to him. He had to keep his feelings under control. He had to stop spending most of his waking hours thinking about her, missing her when she went to work at the pub, and wondering how in hell he was ever going to smooth things over when she found out what he was really after.

She was a tough bird to catch. The toughest. If he'd *really* been serious about marrying her, he'd have made sure she was ready to accept; he'd have been smoother, more persuasive, wouldn't he?

John cursed out loud and acknowledged the truth. He'd have gone about it exactly the way he had. And been rejected.

And been hurt. Absurd! John shook his head, then slapped the Jeep's steering wheel. He'd been a fool for blurting out the stupid proposal.

Following her directions to the newspaper office, John turned the Jeep off a boulevard fronted by the bay, where sailboats and cabin cruisers lolled among shrimp boats. Some were waiting for passage through the Bridge of Lions.

The beauty of Agnes's hometown suddenly made his brooding worse. John whipped the Jeep down a narrow side street crowded with clapboard pastel houses nearly hidden behind flowering trees and vines. Colorful little boutique signs peeked out from their verandas and upper balconies. In the heart of the downtown tourist district it was hard to tell where historic colonial buildings ended and modern copies began.

By the time he located the newspaper office he was so frustrated he slammed the Jeep's front tire against the curb as he parked.

He gritted his teeth and tried to force a cheerful mood as he strode onto the house's white stoop, angling between huge stone pots bursting with red geraniums. He pushed open a narrow white door with *Matanzas Bay Weekly News* painted on the window.

Inside the cheerful little place was a front counter bearing a stack of last week's papers and a bowl of candy. Beyond the counter were several desks topped with computer terminals and other paraphernalia. The walls were covered in framed front pages of special editions. With grim amusement he noted a particular headline.

*Local Ducks Run Afowl of Citizens.*

The room's only occupant was a small brunette woman who looked doll-like in a pink jumpsuit and bright pink earrings. She hopped up from a desk and came quickly to the counter. "You must be John!"

He buried his bad mood and forced what he hoped was a pleasant smile. "John Bartholomew, yes. What gave me away?"

The woman chuckled heartily. "Aggie said you'd be impossible to mistake for anyone else. She was right."

"Did she say it with a dazed expression of bliss on her face or a smirk?"

"She said it while she was chewing a pencil. I couldn't tell."

"You're a very diplomatic lady."

"My name's Meg Gordon. I'm the editor, and I own this beehive of excitement."

"Very pleased to meet you." He had his mood under control now, mostly because he was eager to see Agnes. He glanced toward an open door into a back room. "Is Agnes here?"

"She just ran out to buy a baseball bat. She'll be right back."

After giving her a startled look, John leaned slowly on the counter and brushed a piece of lint from his white coat sleeve. Life with Agnes would never be boring. With exaggerated drama he shook his head and sighed. "I love women who carry sports equipment on their dinner dates."

Meg Gordon's eyes sparkled. "Aggie said nothing could rattle you. She was right."

"I shouldn't ask, but I can't resist. Why did she need a baseball bat?"

"I'll let her explain. She's here."

John straightened quickly and pivoted as the door opened. Despite his bad mood, a deep rush of pleasure ran through him at the sight of her. He felt that way whenever he saw her, even at the ranch, where she seemed determined to hide herself under oversized T-shirts and shorts. What she wore now made him weak in the knees.

It was a minidress with a strapless bodice, made of a bright, delicate flower print. If she stood in one of the city's formal gardens she'd appear to be a luscious red-haired flower herself. John couldn't help admiring her legs for a long moment. Wonderful stems, he wanted to say. Her backless white shoes tilted her up on stiletto heels.

A small white purse hung across her chest, the thin strap angling between her breasts. The strap drew his attention to their smooth, round tops above her bodice. The revealing dress would have been sexy on almost any attractive woman, but on Agnes's plush body it went beyond sexy and defied any red-blooded man to look away.

"I see why you bought the bat," he told her. "For protection."

She had stopped in the doorway as soon as she saw him, and she still stood there, one hand on the door-knob, one hand wrapped around the bat's handle, her gaze riveted to him. She looked as shocked as he. "Nice suit," she said finally, her voice husky. "Nice shirt too."

He touched the dark blue shirt's buttoned collar. "No tie. I hope that's acceptable at local restaurants?"

"Sure." She began shaking her head and smiling.

"What's wrong?"

"Nothing. I'm just thinking that I may need this bat to protect *you*. Gangs of vacationing women roam these streets, you know. They might toss a beach blanket over you and carry you off."

He laughed. Slapping the counter behind John to draw attention to herself and the real world, Meg Gordon announced her good-byes then turned off the over-head light and left through the back door, chuckling under her breath.

"Meg's never seen me this way," Agnes explained as she and John faced each other alone in the office's deep twilight shadows.

"Dressed to delight a man? Good. I like to think you've never worn that dress for anyone but me."

"Sorry, but I borrowed it from my boss at the pub. From his girlfriend, that is. It's been on so many hot dates that the zipper's melted. She was a busy lady before she settled down with Oscar."

"I'm glad you warned me. If any strangers thank you for giving them a good time, I'll tell them they're mistaken."

"Oh, so I'm not a good time?"

He put a hand over his heart. "Agnes, any time I'm with you is a good time."

"Watch the wise-guy attitude. I'm armed." She waggled the bat a little.

"Please explain. I've wrestled with my polite curiosity long enough."

"When I made our dinner reservation, I promised to bring a toy for the Business Club's charity raffle. The restaurant's owner is in charge. He's a pal of mine."

"You know everyone around here, don't you?"

She shrugged. "I've sold horses to people, done stories for the newspaper, that sort of stuff. I get around. This is still a small town in some ways. The shop and restaurant people are a close-knit bunch."

"I like the friendliness here."

"You'd fit in if you, well, that's beside the point. We're gonna be late if we don't get going." She gestured toward the street. "After you. Hmmm, I really love your white suit. You look like a suave jewel thief hanging out in Casablanca."

"Wait." They were already halfway out the door when he stopped her, sliding his fingers gently around her arm. The warm, naked contact nearly drowned him in desire. John knew from the catch in her breath and the way she looked up at him, he wasn't alone. "What were you going to say about me fitting in here?"

"It doesn't matter. You're not gonna stay."

"But I'd fit in if I did? You really think so?"

"Of course. But I was talking without my brain in gear. I know you can't stay."

"And you couldn't come to England for a visit?"

"No."

"Yes you could. If you wanted to."

Her brows shot up in surprise. "I can't leave what I've got here. The ranch is the only thing I've ever owned by myself and for myself. I'm going to make it a success any way I can. Have to, so I'll know that I'm capable of running my own life and doing a good job at it."

*I'm going to make it a success any way I can.* John

thought of the medieval books and what their selling price must mean to her. She'd never give them up without a fight. He wanted to pull her to him and demand she admit having them hidden somewhere. Instead he grasped her shoulders lightly and struggled for composure.

"Don't frown at me," she ordered. "One of us has to be a hard-nosed realist."

He looked over her head into the dusk, wishing he could tell her he'd been one all his life, and would rather capture a few fantasies. The moon had already begun showering the narrow street with light. "It's too pretty a night to talk about depressing subjects," he said gruffly. "Or to wonder about what either of us is going to do next."

After a moment she answered in a subdued voice, "You're right. Feel like walking? It's only a couple of blocks."

"Let's walk, yes. It clears the cobwebs." He gestured toward the bat. "May I carry your war club?"

"Of course."

He grasped it by the handle and held it beside him with his arm slightly flexed. As they started up the deserted street he realized he was watching narrow alleys between houses and gripping the bat with menace. It was an old habit from walking too many dangerous London streets, a habit he'd probably never shake.

If Agnes only knew how stark and unsentimental his world had been, how much he'd tried to change it, and how it had betrayed him! Then she'd understand his fierce reasons for demanding what belonged to him.

But would she understand why he'd deceived her to get it?

Brooding again, he was silent as they turned down a pretty little back street of darkened shops and dim street lamps. The street was paved unevenly in gray bricks flecked with crushed shell. Small, tactful signs said it was closed to car traffic. Thousands of strolling visitors had worn the bricks smooth during the years.

Aggie stumbled on the bumpy surface, and he caught her arm. "Thanks," she said softly. He slid his hand down, unable to resist touching her. She didn't protest when he wound his fingers through hers. Without looking at each other, they held hands and continued walking.

"I feel like a caveman," he quipped. "I have a club in one hand and a woman in the other."

"I can't picture you fighting a saber-toothed tiger. Offering it a cup of tea, maybe."

He forced a laugh and nodded in agreement. "Good tea is a civilizing weapon."

They reached a narrow alley between two old wooden buildings painted pink and white. Overhead was a trellis covered in grapevines. The alley made a pretty little arbor, with a grassy floor. "Let's go through here," she said, tugging John inside. "A shortcut."

John was intrigued with the green tunnel draped in darkness and moonlight. At the other end was a large, well-lighted street, and beyond that were formal gardens of shrubs and palms in front of a cathedral-like stone mansion, one of the city's museums.

She halted him halfway through the arbor, and he gazed down at her, his senses swimming. This was lovely and private, yes, perfect for whatever she had in mind. What he *definitely* had in mind.

"See how the moonlight comes down between the grape leaves," she told him, pointing at the ground. "It makes silver patterns on the grass."

"I like the way it highlights your face."

Slowly she tilted her face up to him. Her hand wound tighter into his. He felt her sudden awkwardness as well as her temptation.

"I'm not going to kiss you," he told her with a hint of victory. He'd challenge her. Agnes couldn't resist a dare.

"You'll have to kiss me first. You'll have to admit you've been planning to kiss me again all along. You've demonstrated fantastic willpower in the past week, and so have I."

Her uneven breath shattered the quiet. "I haven't been planning anything. That's the problem. I never know what I'm going to do next around you. It's frightening."

"Or exciting, if you'll relax."

"You want to hear a secret? If I didn't think you were so special, getting involved would be easier."

"That makes no sense."

"Oh, yes it does. It'd be easier to forget someone ordinary. I've got enough emotional baggage to carry around. I don't want to miss you when you go home."

"You're being a coward. Worse than that, you're taking advantage of me, and I don't like it." His voice was soft but grim. He tossed the baseball bat on the ground and took both her hands in his. "You're using me, Agnes."

Her light gasp echoed off the arbor's close wooden walls. "Using you? In what way?"

"The term 'gentleman' is made of two words. The second is 'man,' with all the deep feelings and desires that implies. I don't expect you to throw yourself at me, but I want you to know that you can't treat me like a harmless pet dog either."

"I never realized I was doing that." Her voice broke, and he could see the distress on her shadowed face. "I'm so sorry. I keep telling myself to stay neutral toward you, but I'm not doing a good job at it."

"No, you're not. But I suppose it's not every day that a stranger invades your life and refuses to leave." He stepped back from her, kissed her hand, then let it go. Letting go was the last thing he wanted to do, but he wouldn't pressure her. He nodded toward their destination. "Onward. My lecture's finished. I've made my point. Think about it."

John started to retrieve the baseball bat from the ground. Right now he felt like bashing it against the wall a few times. Agnes grasped his shoulder. "Wait. Look at me again." Her voice was tortured. "Please."

John straightened slowly. Hurting her bothered him. He cleared his throat roughly. "Let's go to dinner, Agnes. We can talk about this more later."

"No." Suddenly she wound her arms around his neck and rose on her toes. Before he could blink she was giving him a deep and thorough kiss, moving her mouth slowly over his and stroking the back of his head with her fingertips.

He shuddered at the surprise attack and wrapped his arms around her pulling her tighter against him. "I didn't expect this kind of apology," he managed to whisper when she let him breathe again. "I don't want your guilt, I want your passion."

"One provoked the other. But the passion took over. Sssh." Then she returned to kissing him, captivating him with her slow, loving style.

John bent her backward over the crook of his arm and buried himself in her affection, stroking her tongue with his own, twisting his lips to meet her eager attention.

Her breasts were soft globes against him. He slid a hand up her back until it reached the bare skin above the dress's bodice. Her hair was a mass of curls that tickled his palm; he lifted it and caressed the smooth hollow between her shoulder blades.

Deftly she unbuttoned the collar of his shirt. Heat raced through his blood as her nimble fingers stroked his throat. She unfastened several more buttons as he pulled her upright and watched her, his hands now sliding up and down her back.

Breathing quickly, she put her hands inside his shirt

and molded them to his upper chest, exploring him with her palms and fingers. When she dipped her head and began nuzzling the hair, then kissing the center of his chest and working her way upward by tiny degrees, he pushed her gently against the nearest wall and pressed himself to her.

"Yes," she whispered, her lips brushing the front of his throat.

John kissed her hair. The darkness surrounded them and the moonlight feathered down on the fiery red curls. He wound his hands through them and slowly rotated his hips into her yielding belly. Giving a small moan of pleasure, she put her arms around his neck again and lifted her mouth to his.

They swayed together, struggling sensually against the creaking clapboard wall behind them. The motion of his body made her brace her legs apart and let him rest closer to her center. John thought he'd die with pleasure from the deep, hidden pulse between him and her.

He caressed her outer thighs at the edge of the dress's hem. She stroked his back, moving her hands down until they rested on his hips, then urging him to flex into her softness. Slowly he drew her dress upward. The knowledge that they were tempting each other to be reckless in a public place made every action more seductive and forbidden.

Her sighs were rich and trusting in his ears; he wanted to please her even more than himself. And there was a sense of being her protective partner. Her defender. *Her knight*, he thought.

She caught one of his hands and brought it to her breasts. John smiled against her lips as she kissed him again. First he stroked his fingers over the bodice of the dress, then, gauging the encouragement in her trembling body, reached behind her and grasped the dress's zipper.

She made a sound of surprise in her throat but

trembled harder against him. Slowly he slid the zipper down. The bodice sagged loosely around her torso. Whispering his name into the crook of his neck, she raised her arms a little to help him push the material down.

It crumpled into a stiff bundle around her waist, and above it in the moonlight, as she leaned back, her breasts jutted forward delicately. Their white skin looked soft and silvery.

John leaned forward and murmured his admiration into her ear. She made a whimpering sound low in her throat. "Please touch me."

Putting his spread hands over her breasts, he lightly scrubbed his thumbs over the peaks. He felt her knees buckle. John swept one arm under her hips and lifted her high off the ground. She caught his shoulders, and her head draped back. He bent over her erotically upthrust breasts and sucked each one, alternating between roughness and exquisite tenderness. He bit her carefully, heard her make a mewling sound of pleasure, then heard it again when he fathered his tongue over each nipple.

He tantalized her until she began begging him to stop. "You're making me feel faint. I'm breathing too fast," she explained, chuckling weakly. As soon as her feet touched the ground she sagged against him and took his mouth with a new series of devastating kisses.

Her hands moved down his body, feathering over his exposed chest, caressing his sides, then brushing across the fashionable pleats along the front of his white trousers. When he trembled under her stroking hands she cupped them gently over him, tracing him through the material with her fingertips.

"Oh, Mr. Bartholomew," she whispered raggedly. "You're fantastic."

He wanted to whirl her around in a circle and shout to the world that he'd found the sexiest, most loving woman in the world. But nothing was more important than putting his arms around her again and holding her warmly, stroking her naked back.

John curved his hands over her rump and memorized her curves with his palms. She curled against him and wrapped her arms around his waist. Her hard nipples tantalized him through his shirt, and the quick, helpless rhythm of her breathing aroused him to more desire as well as a new, more fervent intention to make every moment special for her.

He curled a hand under the hem of her dress, lifted it, then cupped her bottom. Sleek pantyhose made her thighs feel like warm, polished porcelain. Inside their practical cover she was dissolving into elemental feminine need for him, and he knew it. He slipped his fingers between her thighs and stroked her through the sheer covering.

She whimpered, then arched against him and buried her face in his shoulder, murmuring his name over and over. Shaken at the power of her response, he lowered her skirt and cradled her in his arms again, rocking her a little. A gentleman probably shouldn't tell her that he'd like to rip her pantyhose apart, lift her legs around his waist, and take her with her back buried in grapevines and the rough boards of a wall scrubbing her shoulders.

After a minute she drew her head up and looked at him. They couldn't see each other well in the shadowy moonlight, but he knew she was happy. He felt the edges of her smile when he kissed each of her warm, damp cheeks.

She rested her forehead against his. He grasped her hands and brought them up again, then cupped her palms along his jaw. While she stroked his cheeks he pulled her bodice into place and deftly slid his hands around her back, then zipped her dress up.

"Aren't women the lucky ones," he teased in a hoarse voice. "No one can tell what they've been doing. But we men are different. We have to stop before our, uhmm, *affection* becomes impossible to hide."

"It's all right to be shy," she said, and kissed him tenderly. "I understand. I've never done anything like this in public before either."

No, she didn't understand, John thought mildly. He was ready, willing, and able to make love to her right there, and he'd never been shy about sex.

"I want to learn everything about your body," he told her, stroking her face with the back of his fingers. "Let's not hurry even one second of intimacy. It's too precious."

She cried out poignantly and kissed him until he thought he'd lose his mind from wanting her. He pulled her tighter against him. "I want to sit across a restaurant table from you and watch you be very polite, while I think about what we were doing in this arbor and watch *you* think about it."

"I'll have to play footsies with you under the table. I won't be able to control myself."

"I'll encourage your feet to be bad, very bad. Agnes, I have to warn you—by the time dinner ends, your feet will be in ecstasy."

"Let's go! My toes are curling already." They laughed softly. He'd never known such a poignant combination of tenderness and humor before. They held each other close and didn't talk anymore, letting the white-hot needs cool down, while the affection burned even brighter.

He relaxed, shut his eyes, and nuzzled his face into her hair. She tucked her head close to his and sighed happily. Agnes made him forget that he'd ever been anyone but the man he'd created for her. He was beginning to like that image of himself a lot. Perhaps he really *was* as gentlemanly and civilized as she thought. He shared a perfect cocoon of contentment with her.

Until someone poked a gun into his back.

# *Seven*

Aggie sat stiffly in the police detective's office, feeling numb. Only her fierce willpower kept her from jumping up and going to find John. Sure, the police were right to have a paramedic check him out. It was good public relations policy for the police to pamper a visitor who'd been mugged.

But she suspected they also wanted to separate her from John and ask more questions about the incident. She forced herself to be calm, even though she hadn't finished sorting out what had happened. Plus the setting brought back wrenching memories of the investigation following Richard's arrest.

Aggie exhaled raggedly and clenched her hands around her purse. She couldn't blame them for being curious, not when the muggers were three swaggering beach-bum types with criminal records, and John had put all three into the hospital.

She stifled a giddy, exhausted laugh with no humor in it. She was thinking she'd have to buy a new baseball bat for the Business Club's charity raffle. The other one had blood stains.

Detective Herberts entered and sat down at his desk. He was as compulsively neat as his office, without a stain on his gold tie or a stray tuft in his cropped brown hair. His smooth, round face had a smug expression that said he never let a detail escape. Smiling thinly, he pulled a notepad toward him and began writing.

"How long have you known Mr. Bartholomew?"

"About a week and a half. He's a guest at my campground."

"He says he owns a chain of hobby shops in London. Is that what he told you?"

"Yes."

Herberts read a London address to her. "That's the address on his passport. Do you have any reason to doubt it?"

Astonished, she shook her head. "Why are you asking about all this?"

"Just curious. We don't get a tourist like him every day."

*Or every century,* she thought. "What do you mean?"

Herberts ticked off points on his slender, tanned fingers. "Broken noses. Cracked ribs. Concussions. One ruptured spleen. One fractured wrist. That's what he did to three men who had reputations for being pretty damned dangerous, pardon my language. What I'm saying, Ms. Hamilton, is your average citizen doesn't methodically beat muggers to a pulp."

Aggie leaned forward furiously, glaring at him. "What was John supposed to do? One of them had a gun! The others had knives!"

"Granted, they don't deserve any sympathy. But don't you see what I'm getting at? You heard him when he was describing what happened. Most victims of a mugging can't remember a tenth of the details. Can you?"

"But it all happened so fast!"

"Then why could Mr. Bartholomew remember specifics?"

"He stayed calm, that's why. He was cooperating,

tellin' them he'd hand over his wallet, until one of them grabbed me."

"Okay. What happened next?"

She ran her fingers through her hair, trying to remember. It *was* odd that John had been able to recall everything so accurately. As if fighting in alleys was something he did every day. Aggie shook her head. "He kicked the one who had the gun."

"Where did he kick him?"

"Right between the legs. Hard. With the side of his foot."

"As if he were trained in martial arts?"

"I guess. It all happened too fast for me to wonder if John was doing a Kung Fu act. The next thing I knew, he picked up the baseball bat, and those three bastards began figuring out they'd picked the wrong man to rob."

"Has he ever said anything to you about his past? Any training in self-defense?"

Frowning, she shook her head. "But I, uh, think he was pretty good at fencing, when he was in prep school." Herberts rolled his eyes, and her face burned. "You know, fencing? Two people poke at each other with thin little sabers? Then they shake hands and go to tea, I think." She made herself grin at him, trying to lighten the interrogation.

Herberts didn't crack a smile. "Maybe Mr. Bartholomew ought to offer his batting skills to a major-league baseball team. Or join a street gang."

Aggie's stomach twisted sickly and her patience ran out. She stood. "I think you'd be happier if he'd let those jerks rob us, beat us up, and maybe rape me for the heck of it."

"Calm down. It's my job to be thorough."

"You've done your job. Now John and I are gettin' out of here. We're not in any trouble, and I don't know why you think it's odd for a man to react the way John did."

Herberts stood rigidly. "Thank you for your coopera-
tion. Good night."

She stalked out.

In the front lobby, John slung his coat over one arm
and shoved his hands into his trousers pockets, disre-
garding the pain in his lightly bandaged knuckles. He
was oblivious to everything except his own dark thoughts
about what he'd done and how Agnes might be reacting
to it.

He kept imagining what could have happened to her if
he hadn't taken action. Cold shivers ran through him.
He'd never had to defend anyone other than himself
before.

After he'd kicked the man with the gun he'd slammed
a fist into his face. The man had dropped instantly, and
John had gone after the other two. He'd been dimly
aware of the first man moving sluggishly on the ground
and Agnes dropping on top of him like a ferocious cat.
When he finished with the others John whirled toward
the two of them, ready to kill the man if he'd hurt her.

But the half-conscious attacker was moaning and
shivering as Agnes threatened him with her shoes,
which she held in her hands. She'd seated herself on
him and stuck the tip of a sharp high-heel into each of
his ears. Her intent was clear—one wrong move and
he'd need a surgeon to remove the shoes from his head.

"You got 'em, John, you got 'em!" she'd proclaimed
excitedly. He'd never forget the look on her face as she'd
gazed up at him. Pride and devotion had glowed in her
eyes. Her hair was tousled, and strands clung to her
cheeks like tendrils of fire.

The love he'd tried so hard to ignore had filled him
suddenly and so richly that he'd dropped the baseball
bat, gone to her swiftly, lifted her up from the half-
conscious mugger, and kissed her. And she'd kissed
him back, then smiled. *Smiled*, standing in a dark

arbor with her lethal shoes clutched in her hands, and three bloodied men lying around her feet.

There was no other woman in the world like her. He'd known that before, but now he admitted it.

When he heard her sharp little shoes on the hallway tile of the police station he turned swiftly. She and he met halfway across the lobby. She looked flushed and a little grim, but threw her arms around his neck and hugged him hard. "Are you all right?" he asked hoarsely.

"Yes." She looked at him in surprise. "The detective just asked me some questions. Are you okay?"

"Fine."

"Fine," she mocked lightly, her voice catching. She slung her purse strap over one shoulder and quickly took his injured hand in both of hers. "What did the paramedic say?"

"That I should keep my caveman impulses under control until my knuckles heal."

She shook her head firmly. "Don't talk that way. I'm proud of what you did."

"Are you? When we arrived here you were staring at me as if you'd never seen me before."

"Nobody's every defended my honor before. I'm in a daze. And frankly, I was worried. You seemed sort of aloof, or withdrawn."

"Aloof? All I've been thinking about is you. But you seemed to need some privacy to absorb what happened and decide how you feel about me."

"I'm sorry. Being here makes me a little crazy, because of what I went through with Richard. It's been more than five years, but I don't think I'll ever be comfortable in a police station again. I know it's irrational, but I feel ashamed and guilty, even though I didn't do anything wrong, then or now."

He hugged her tightly. "What did the detective ask you?"

"He wanted to know what your batting average is." At John's puzzled frown she added seriously, "He thinks it's strange that a Mr. Nice Guy like you could fight back so well. He wondered if you'd had martial arts training. I told him no." She cocked her head and eyed John curiously. "Have you? You and I have talked a lot about our lives in the past week, but there's a lot I don't know."

"You know me well enough to trust me, I hope."

Aggie gazed up into his sleekly carved face, the face that had attracted but unnerved her from the beginning. The slant of the thick eyebrows, the flaring nostrils, the dark eyes and wide, seductive mouth could have been hard and frightening, but not to her. Maybe there was some mystery behind his eyes, but it meant nothing compared to the courage there.

His dark hair had furrows in it as if he'd been raking his fingers through the thick strands, and his eyes were fierce with concern. He looked depressed, and she couldn't understand why. "You did the right thing tonight," she told him softly.

"But it was ugly. I'm sorry you saw me that way."

"John, I love your gallant ideas about protecting my ideals, but don't worry so much. I wasn't disgusted by what you did. We're both alive and unhurt because of you. Think of me this way—I'm as tough as one of those medieval women who supervised the crops, doctored the sick, made the family's clothes, and went hunting when she needed meat for the dinner table. You can treat me like the lady of the castle, but Lady Agnes is no wimp, Sir John."

His face tightened at her whimsical lecture. He looked almost angry. "I know I did the right thing, but I don't want you to think I have a dark side I never told you about."

She caught his face between her hands and gave him a kiss, despite the watchful gaze of a sergeant at the desk across the room. "We gotta stop making out in public places." Aggie swallowed a knot of emotion in her throat.

The affection in his eyes warmed her. "Let's go home, then."

She nodded happily. *Home.* She loved the way he included himself in it. He held out his good hand and she grasped it. As they left the police station it occurred to her, he hadn't answered her question about martial arts. Oh, it wasn't important, anyway. She knew all she needed to know about him and had never been so confident before in her life. She loved him desperately.

His past was catching up with him, not in a way other people could notice but inside him, because the half-truths he'd let Agnes believe about himself were a black shadow on their future. John watched pensively as she crossed her living room to switch on a window air conditioner.

He clenched his bruised hand and hardly felt the pain. He had to merge the John Bartholomew she knew with the man he really was, the man who'd demonstrated the difference blatantly tonight. She not only still trusted him, she trusted him completely. To her there was nothing strange about a proper British businessman suddenly doing a switch worthy of Dr. Jekyll and Mr. Hyde.

*Mr. Hyde isn't a monster*, he wanted to tell her. *He's even won some awards for public service. He's honest and loyal, despite evidence to the contrary.*

"John?" She came to him and took his hands, studying him anxiously. "Come sit down. You look worn out and upset."

"I didn't enjoy hurting those men. But it couldn't be helped."

"Sssh. Stop explaining to me. I understand." She led him to the comfortably sprung chintz couch, tossed his coat aside, then lightly pushed him down into the couch's corner. "Lean back." She stuffed throw pillows behind his head, then propped his feet on an ottoman she pulled from under a lamp table. Quickly she removed his soft camel-colored loafers. "There. Are you hungry?"

"Not really."

"I know what'll be good! Be right back." He had to smile. Agnes was unstoppable. Five minutes later she returned from the kitchen with a bowl of vanilla ice cream and a tall frosted glass rattling with ice. "Sugar and liquor," she intoned wickedly.

John sank deeper into the cushions and chuckled. Her inventive attention delighted him. Sipping a stiff gin and tonic, he watched her curl up beside him. She fed him a spoonful of ice cream, and its coolness followed the liquor's fiery path down his throat. "Wonderful," he admitted.

"I thought you'd like it. By the time you finish all this you'll be under my spell."

"That sounds intriguing. Then what?"

"Oh, I don't know. Let's be spontaneous." She fed him more ice cream. He downed half of his drink in a deep swallow then gazed at her through half-shut eyes, a purposeful little smile on his lips. He wanted her to love him. That was the first step toward making things right. "What can I do for you, Agnes?" he asked in thick whisper, the gin relaxing his throat.

She stroked her fingertips across his forehead. Tears glistened in her eyes, but she looked serene. "Enjoy yourself," she answered. "I'm going to make you feel better." She dabbed the smooth vanilla on the cleft of his lips, leaned forward quickly, and licked it away with the tip of her tongue.

Languid desire wound through him. He felt weighted to the couch. His heart was beating faster, and his skin was hot and sensitive. He kissed her hand. "There's lazy, tired sultan in my head who'd love to lounge here and let you play harem slave. But that's not fair to you. You're tired too."

Slipping another spoonful of ice cream into his mouth, she shook her head. The seduction in her eyes made the ice cream melt on his tongue. 'Don't be a gentleman tonight," she commanded in a husky tone. "And I won't be a lady."

The breath soughed out of him. She winked and got up from the couch. "What are you leaving for?" She was already halfway down the hall to her bedroom.

"To put on my harem outfit."

John set the dishes on an end table, laid his head back on the pillows and shut his eyes, his thoughts whirling. He'd won her trust. Could he win her love?

Aggie stripped off her clothes and, going to her bedroom closet, took out a pearl-gray silk robe she'd bought after her divorce to cheer herself up but had never worn, until tonight. Her knees quivered, but she wasn't nervous. Her body hummed with tenderness and arousal. Touching her nipples, she sighed at their heavy, strutted excitement.

She carried a damp washcloth with her when she returned to the living room. John lifted his head as she sat down beside him again. The admiration in his dark eyes scorched her. Slowly their gaze moved down the robe's sheer surface to the black tie-belt at her waist. She'd arranged the lapels to show a vee of pale skin down the center of her chest.

Her breath shuddered when he reached over and brushed a fingertip across the tiny beauty mark between her breasts. "A lovely landmark for wayward travelers."

"You have a way with words." She knelt on the couch and began gently cleaning his face with the cloth. With her other hand she unbuttoned his shirt down to the slim leather belt at the waist of his white trousers. Her eyes met his as she pulled the shirt open and ran the warm, wet cloth in slow circles on his chest.

His face was flushed and had a primitive look of hunger along with the slightest hint of a smile, which made her realize this languid tiger was patiently waiting to eat her up. The danger in him still shows, she thought with a hot rush of pleasure.

Some people used that kind of emotional power as a weapon. Richard had. Her parents too. But with John she shared a sense of security and partnership. Their backgrounds had nothing in common, but he seemed to understand her problems and needs.

Aggie's fingers trembled with desire as she unfastened his belt and trousers. His quiver of response aroused her even more as she smoothed the cloth over his belly and the hard welcome there.

Curling her arms around his legs, she bent forward and placed kisses on that eager, intimate part of his body. His hands sank convulsively into her hair and his back arched. His pleasure sang in her blood.

She tantalized him slowly, listening to his soft baritone murmurs of encouragement, half-formed words mingling with the heavy rhythm of his breath. Suddenly he gave a harsh groan of restraint and pulled her up to him. She lay across his chest, her robe wrenched open, as his hands stroked and squeezed her breasts. He kissed her roughly, and she clung to him.

Seconds later they were both naked and stretched out on the couch, winding themselves around each other. Aggie curved her hand down the sloping muscles of his back and sighed with pleasure when he slipped his leg deeply between hers. She gripped him with her thighs. He pulled her against him and flexed enticingly. Aggie was quivering with sensation.

She encouraged him wildly, lapping her tongue into his mouth, loving the taste of vanilla and gin. John reached over her and pulled his coat from the back of the couch. It tumbled down on them, smooth and inviting on her skin.

He retrieved something from an inside pocket then tickled the slim soft edge up her arm. Aggie lifted her head to look at the plastic packet. They traded a quiet, serious gaze as he brushed it across her lips. "I bought a few of these today."

Aggie kissed the packet and nodded, satisfied. He was as perfect as she'd expected. "I bought some today too," she admitted. "I told you that I never know what'll happen next between you and me. I decided to be ready."

She prepared him with slow, provocative hands, while he sank his fingers into her hair and kissed her. Then he knelt between her knees and pressed her onto her back atop the comfortable cushions. His gaze holding hers intensely, he stretched out on her deeper and deeper until suddenly he was inside her. Her moan of delight made a keening sound.

"My lady, you're humming like a bell that's just been rung," he whispered against her ear. Aggie wound her arms and legs around him. An ecstatic laugh bubbled in her throat. "Oh, how well you do the ringing, Sir John."

Smiling, he put his mouth on hers, stopped the laugh, and took the last of her control away with his body's movements. She whispered his name as if it were the soft, sweet echo of a timeless song.


John stood in her dark office, a glass of milk in his hand, a pair of shorts hanging, half-fastened, on his hips.

Her old rolltop desk looked ridiculously easy to open. The drawer locks wouldn't last a minute when he coaxed them with the slender metal pick he kept in his backpack. When Agnes went to work at the pub Thursday night, he'd pop the drawers and check their contents.

Maybe she didn't have the books. He had to find out, then decide how to tell her why he'd come here. If she didn't have them, he still wouldn't have an easy time explaining himself. But dammit, he'd convince her, somehow, that the books were a separate problem and had nothing to do with his feelings for her.

He scrutinized the books and papers stacked on the desk. She'd put all her medieval textbooks and notes away. All he saw now were veterinary manuals and forms to be filled out on the new colt so he'd be confirmed by the country's official registry for purebred quarter horses.

John idly toyed with the ceramic vase holding a silk begonia while he burned inside with grim speculation. Had Agnes deliberately hidden the evidence from him? He'd never given her any reason to worry about his motives. Maybe she didn't trust him as much as he thought.

John angrily thumped the vase. As it had the other time he'd disturbed it, the vase rattled inside. Quickly he turned it upside down, jabbing his fingers into the fake begonias so they wouldn't spill.

A tiny, rusty key fell out.

His breath rough in his throat, he inserted the key into the desk's top drawer, tested it, and felt the lock click. He had a dull sense of victory. Agnes wasn't very good at hiding things. Not exactly skilled in the sleazier arts of deception, the way he was.

Or maybe she'd believed him too decent and honorable to look through her desk. John locked the drawer without opening it, tossed the key into the vase, and left the room.

Still carrying his glass of milk, he returned to her bedroom. John scowled at the glass and mocked himself. Wholesome, yeah. He halted at the foot of the bed, and watched Agnes sleep. She was an enticing pale shape half covered by the sheets. She lay on her back with one hand unfurled over her breasts and the other tossed aside on his empty pillow.

He promised her silently that he wasn't going to steal from her or hurt her in any way.

She shifted, stretching sleepily, her body as supple as a dozing cat's. The thin white sheet accentuated the inviting sight. Bittersweet desire and concern almost made him dizzy.

Her hand feathered over his pillow. She rose on one elbow and looked around groggily. "John?" He went to the side of the bed and knelt, stroking a hand over her hair. "Sssh. I'm right here. I went for a glass of milk. I have to keep my strength up, you know."

"Hmmm. Keep it up." She lightly ran her hand over his chest, as if reassuring herself that he was real. "Hmmm." Her fingertips tickled their way down his belly and found his unzipped shorts. "Hmmm."

John inhaled sharply. "My milk is turning into a milkshake." He held the glass to her mouth and she took a sip. "I have a cow mustache," she told him, chuckling.

John set the glass on the nightstand, bent over her, and took her face between his hands. He licked the crest of milk from her upper lip. "All gone."

"Too bad." She curled her arms around his neck and nuzzled her nose to his. Then she said his name tenderly. "This night makes a whole lifetime of loneliness seem worth it."

John retrieved the glass of milk, pushed the sheet off her, and began kissing her thighs. He tilted the glass over them and trickled milk into the fluffy auburn hair at their center.

She gasped. "We'll have to change the bed!" But her voice was breathless.

"I won't let one drop escape," he promised, catching the milk with his tongue.


"Whatzit?" Oscar demanded as soon as she walked into the pub on Thursday evening. A few tourists were eating sandwiches at the big, rustic tables covered in checkered vinyl cloths; the pub was an after-dinner hangout, and the crowd wouldn't arrive for about an hour.

Aggie grinned at him mysteriously and began tying a white apron around her white shorts. She made an X over the center of her bright-red blouse. "Cross your heart and promise not to tease me?"

"Got no heart." Oscar made an X over the midsection of his white T-shirt. "I'll cross my stomach. That's the part I pay the most attention to. Well, almost."

"Close enough." She bounced onto a tall chair behind the bar and swung her feet cheerfully. "I'm in love."

"Yow! The British guy?"

She nodded. "Not just in love, but absolutely crazy about him. Just your basic once-in-a-lifetime kind of thing. Do you think anyone can tell I'm happier than I've ever been before?"

"Have you said all this to him?"

"Not yet."

"He said it to you?"

"Uhmm, not yet." She frowned at Oscar. "We agreed to live in the present. We're takin' things slow. We just met about two weeks ago!"

"Huh. Slow, right. But he's already Mr. Forever." Oscar looked doubtful. "He's gonna love you in the future, but not now?"

She stopped swinging her feet. "Oscar, if anybody ever asks you to play Cupid, break their face."

"Whatza matter? Can't take a little reality?"

"I hate reality." She huffed at Oscar's attitude. "W

agreed this week we'd get to know each other better. *Next* week we'll talk about love, I'm sure."

Oscar pursed his mouth primly. "Getting to know each other, hmmm. As in, Who hogs the covers at night and who's got the most ticklish tummy?"

Aggie gave him her dead-eye-dare look and said drolly, "I guess that's one way of lookin' at it."

"Just asking."

"He's a jewel, Rattinelli. A jewel. I've known a lot of fakes in my life, but John's the real thing. You'll see."

"I hope so." Oscar lumbered away to attend an elderly couple who were impatiently tapping their canes on the bar.

Aggie glared after him. She'd expected congratulations from big-hearted Oscar. He knew her well enough to see that John had made a remarkable change in her attitude. And that wasn't reckless, that was good, dammit. What was wrong with deciding that fantasies could come true?

She glowered at Oscar for the rest of the night.

At closing she looked up from washing bar glasses to find Detective Herberts pushing open the pub's creaky screened door. Aggie stared at him with exasperation but also a sense of dread. Why was he so persistent?

"Got time to serve you one drink," she said brusquely. She gestured at the chairs stacked on tables and the disconnected neon beer signs. Oscar was in the back, checking inventory. "We're rolling up the sidewalks."

"I'm not here for a drink." Herberts settled his tanned, neatly dressed self on a bar stool and studied her somberly. To his credit, he didn't look smug. "I couldn't get over my curiosity about your friend."

"Oh, no, not another interrogation. I'm telling you, John Bartholomew is a classy British businessman with nothing to hide. If the man were any more idealistic, honest, and brave, he'd be locked up in a museum with a plaque that said 'The Only One of His Kind' on it." She shook drops of water off a beer glass and hoped some of them hit Herberts.

The detective sighed. "Oh, he's been locked up, all right, but not in a museum. Until a month ago he was serving time in a London prison."

Herberts had the good grace not to smile when the beer glass shattered on the floor.

# Eight

John sat in the darkened office at Agnes's desk for a long time before he turned on its gooseneck lamp, retrieved the key from the vase of begonias, and unlocked the desk drawers.

In a deep bottom drawer he found the metal security box. He held it on his lap, his nerves tingling. Was there a fortune inside? If there were, had Agnes realized that already? A shiver of awe slid up his spine. Was he holding the diary and prayer book that had belonged to his ancestor more than eight hundred years ago?

He ran his thumbs over the box's lock. Knowing Agnes, the key was probably tucked into a cranny of the desk drawers, easy enough to find if he needed to. But his method would be simpler. He set the box on the desktop, located two gym clips in a plastic cup in one drawer, and bent the clips to suit his purpose.

After a minute of delicate, creative lock-picking, the mechanism popped open. John's pulse hammered in his ears as he lifted the lid.

He'd found them. One book was larger than the other, slightly wider and longer than his spread fingers. The other was a slender volume small enough to cup in one hand.

The leather bindings were faded and bore fine cracks. Still-colorful designs were stamped into the leather, and words in Latin. He realized he was caressing the words with his fingertips. Opening the larger book, he found dark, masculine writing on leaves of yellow parchment. The writing was in Latin, also, but he turned the pages with reverence, as if he understood. This man's blood ran in his veins.

The smaller book contained beautiful artwork in the page corners, and the highly ornamented script probably meant the book had been copied by monks for use in a church library or the private collection of a wealthy noble. Its pages were filled with titled verses. It was obviously Sir Miles's prayer book.

John had never expected to feel as if he'd found something holy and yet very personal. But these books were his link to a family legacy far more noble than any of his family in modern times. He set them on the desk reverently.

Under the books was a thick sheaf of notebook paper bound with a heavy black clip. John thumbed through it, his heart in his throat. The writing was uneven and angular, not Agnes's smooth, looping hand. John realized suddenly that this was the diary's translation. The handwriting was her grandfather's.

But the writing on the small yellow squares of paper stuck to an inside page was definitely Agnes's. John read the notes, disbelieving. Phrases, obviously from Sir Miles's diary, were copied and underlined. *Love and honor are never forgotten. A man is the measure of his heart. To live without honesty is to deny courage.*

And on one slip of paper she'd written "Sir Miles" a dozen times, with pretty flourishes. It was the kind of thing a schoolgirl would do while she daydreamed about a special boy.

Stunned, John stared at the books. Now he understood why she didn't trust him enough to confide about them, the way he'd hoped she would. Sir Miles of Norcross, a hero, a martyr, was the knight in shining armor Agnes wanted.

John shut his eyes and cursed wearily. He'd played right into her fantasy, not realizing that he wasn't winning her with his own gallantry, but with his ancestor's.

She was in love with a man who'd been dead for eight centuries.

He knew he was being a sentimental fool, but it hurt. It hurt because he was no more like his ancestor than a draft horse was like a Thoroughbred. John shoved the books and notes back into the box and thrust it into the drawer.

He left the office with long, angry strides, his mood black. Agnes didn't want to love him, not the real John Bartholomew, and he'd been stupid to ever think she would. Pacing the living room floor, he glared at the couch were they'd first made love. Whom had she been clinging to so wildly—a ghost?

The phone rang in the kitchen. He jerked the receiver from the cradle and coldly snapped a hello.

"It's Mrs. Cranshaw," a tearful little voice said. "From the campground."

"Yeah?" he answered curtly.

"My husband fell. I think he's broken his leg. Please come help us. There's no one else at the campground. Please."

What did she think he was, a doctor? He was tired of playing everyone's saint around here. Tired of acting out Agnes's fantasy. "I'll be there right away," he told Mrs. Cranshaw. He might not be perfect, but he wasn't capable of cruelty either.

"Bless you."

John gentled his voice and told her not to worry, that everything would be all right. He hung up the phone then muttered curses while he scrawled a note to Agnes.

He pounded it to the front door with one well-aimed blow of his palm against a thumb tack.

*I'm no bloody saint,* he thought fiercely, as he threw his Jeep into gear and tore off down the dirt road to the campground. He was still thinking it when he took Mr. Cranshaw to the hospital, and when he spent the rest of the night comforting Mrs. Cranshaw in the waiting room. *No bloody saint.* They'd all better wise up. Especially Agnes.

She found the note when she finally came home, after talking to Detective Herberts for an hour. *Taking Mr. Cranshaw to hospital. Broken leg. Will call you. John.*

Agnes leaned woodenly against the wall under the porch light and stared at John's words while tears slid down her face. As usual, he was playing the gentleman. The rescuer. The brave protector of the needy.

He was a brutal, coldhearted liar.

Her dogs flopped around her, gazing up curiously as they listened to her harsh sobs. They jumped and scattered when she made a guttural sound of pain and fury. Then they followed her to the barn at a lope.

Agnes threw the light switch and halted in the center of the hall, her hands clenched and chest heaving. She'd teach him a lesson as bitter and outrageous as the one he'd taught her. She'd make him admit the truth about who he was and what he wanted, and then she'd make him listen to every blistering word she had to say in response.

John could have the books belonging to his family. He could have his victory, and he could go back to England with a smirk on his face, but he'd never forget her or what she was going to do to him.

Agnes dumped several wheelbarrows of extra wood shavings into a clean stall. She checked the heavy iron eyelet bolted into its back wall. None of the horses that had been tethered there over the years had been able to pull it loose. John Bartholomew, no matter how much of an animal he was, wouldn't stand a chance.

He was half asleep by the time he returned to Agnes's place. Mrs. Cranshaw was comfortably settled at a motel near the hospital, and her husband was doing well. The Cranshaws' grown children were already on their way to Florida to help their parents.

His anger at Agnes sagged. Resignation set in along with the fatigue. He needed her the way the tide needed a shore. He couldn't deny that, even if she didn't love him, even if she looked at him and saw some Sir Lancelot type, straight out of Camelot, instead of a flesh-and-blood, highly fallible man.

Dawn painted her house and barn with a pink mist. The air was cool and tangy. John dragged himself from the Jeep and noticed the barn door was open. Frowning, he shooed the dogs aside and went in. The lights were on. Agnes's palomino mare, Sassy, gazed at him from a stall in the far end.

"Agnes?" he called, frowning. "Are you here?"

There was a rustling sound in one of the stalls. She stumbled out, barefoot, brushing wood shavings from her shorts and shirt. Her hair was disheveled and she rubbed her eyes groggily. From the red, puffy look of her face, she'd been asleep for hours. No wonder she hadn't answered the phone when he'd called. "Mornin'," she said hoarsely. "Cranshaws all right?"

"Yes." He told her what had happened. She nodded. "Thanks for helping them out. You must be exhausted."

He walked up to her, feeling an odd strain in the air but unable to put his finger on the cause. Of course, in his pensive, simmering bad mood, he could be imagining things. "Yes. Why are you out here?"

"Sassy was hanging around alone when I got home

from work. I think she's about to go into labor. She had
a rough time foaling last year. I want to stay close by."
Agnes took his hand. "Come on. I fixed a place in the
stall. Wood shavings make a great bed. Let's go to sleep."

"That's the best suggestion I've heard all night."

She'd spread blankets in one corner of the stall. When
he lay down beside her the deep bed of wood shavings
conformed to his shape like a luxury mattress. "Sweet
man," she whispered, and kissed his cheek. "Want to
take your clothes off? You know how muggy it gets in
here later in the morning."

"That's the *other* best suggestion I've heard all night."

"I'll help." She quickly removed his jogging shoes,
khaki shorts, and short-sleeved white pullover. John
sighed when the pleasant dawn air hit his bare skin. It
was soothing to lie there in nothing but his white
briefs. He felt as if Agnes had stripped away some of his
doubts. His arousal was quick and demanding.

"Whoa, boy," she said, that edgy tone in her voice
again. His imagination? She slapped his stomach playfully, but it stung. John looked at her askance. "Sleep
first, play later," she told him.

"I'm not the spanking type, Agnes." He forced a
chuckle.

"You're a big ol' sweet honey bear. But go to sleep."

Her drawl was heavy as syrup. He wearily recalled
something about her warning him about it. It was a
sign of her dangerous side, she'd said. But what was
dangerous about lying here beside her in nothing but
his briefs, with her hands rubbing his shoulders?

He shut his eyes. Tormented emotions still churned
inside him—sadness and worry and a sense of betrayal
because her feelings for him probably weren't what he
wanted them to be. But when she continued to massage
his shoulders he looked up at her gently. "You really look
like you've been through the wringer." He reached up to
caress her face. "Anything wrong?"

She pulled back, shook her head, but smiled. "If you touch me like that I'll pounce on you. But it might be painful."

He chuckled sleepily and dropped his hand to his side. "Lie down and snuggle with me."

"Yum. But let me take care of you first." She tossed his clothes to a far corner of the stall then began rubbing tiny circles on his forehead, her fingertips coaxing tendrils of sleep through his brain. He shut his eyes and told himself he'd try to make sense of what Agnes wanted from him later, when his mind was fresh.

She bent over him as he drifted into darkness. "Relax and let yourself go," she crooned, massaging his temples. "And when you wake up you'll think you're a new man."

*Maybe you can love him,* John thought just before he fell asleep.


Agnes stood in the stall's far corner and watched him wake up. He was covered in sweat, but not from the barn's noonday temperature. The fan she'd set in the stall's open doorway made a nice breeze.

She hoped he was having a nightmare.

His muscular, nearly naked body was restless on the blankets. He rubbed one brawny hand across his face, raked it over his black hair, and grimaced savagely with his eyes still shut.

She shivered and hugged herself. His rough, unpredictable nature showed when he slept. She should have noticed before, but she'd been blind.

His eyes opened abruptly and he bolted upright, breathing hard and squinting in the sunlight that came through a big screened window. "Sleep well?" she asked in an acid tone.

But he missed the change in attitude and answered groggily, "I was dreaming about being choked. Strangest dream . . ." He halted. His big, commanding hands flew to the thick chain padlocked snugly around his neck.

His astonished gaze shot to her bitter one. "Are we being kinky, Agnes?"

"No. We're being realistic. You're vicious. I chained you up like a rabid dog."

He grabbed the chain where it trailed down the front of his chest, stared at it in shock, then swiveled on his rump and noted the chain's path to the wall, where its other end was padlocked to the iron eyelet. The chain was long enough for him to move around the corner even stand up if he wanted to, but nothing else. Agnes watched him with sharp misery.

He turned toward her again, searching her face for answers. She didn't say a word. Neither did he. Finally she saw the explanation sink in. For a moment his expression was suffused with emotions that shocked her. She wouldn't believe they were sorrow and pain.

He shut his eyes. His jaw clenched hard, and sinews stood out along his neck. But when he opened his eyes he was suddenly in control, and a cold, harsh sheen had dropped over his gaze. Her knees went weak. Was she meeting the real John Bartholomew for the first time?

"How did you find out?" he asked. Even his voice had changed. Its cultured tones had a hard, streetwise edge It mocked his story about having a London town house and hinted at where he really lived, a cheap apartment above an escort service. He might as well live over a brothel, Detective Herberts had told her.

"Your lies caught up with you." She described her conversation with Herberts.

Disgust flared in John's eyes. "He told you the truth But he doesn't know the whole truth."

"The truth, the whole truth, and nothing but the truth, so help me God," she recited in a flat, bitter tone "That's what I want from you."

"No, you don't. You've already made up your mind."

"You lied to me. You used me." Her legs collapsed and she sat down weakly in the corner. She wanted to sob again, but fury kept her back rigid and her chin up. "You didn't go to Oxford, you weren't on the British Olympic equestrian team, and you sure don't own any hobby stores. So introduce yourself. I want to meet Scotland Yard's Inspector Bartholomew."

He inhaled sharply. "Be accurate. Ex-inspector. Ex-convict. Sent to prison for three months last year for taking bribes from the terrorist groups I was supposed to be spying on. I can see the distrust on your face—everything you think you know about me, and everything you hate."

"I hate lies. I hate being deceived. I hate going to bed with a man who was using me the way he'd use one of his downstairs neighbors from the so-called escort service."

"You find it pretty damned easy to jump to conclusions about me and my habits. And about what I was 'using' you for. You hate lies, well, so do I. But I also hate losing my inheritance to a thieving American army captain who took advantage of my grandparents during World War Two."

"That's not what happened!"

"I'm willing to give you a chance to explain. More than you'll give me."

"You lied to me about everything in your background. I've never been anything but honest with you. That's the difference between me trusting you and you trusting me."

"Honest? Then why didn't you tell me about the books hidden in your desk?"

"I would have, soon! I've been scared to tell *anyone*!" She gasped as she realized how he knew where they were located. "You went through my desk!"

His hard, unwavering gaze told her yes, he had. Aggie

leaned back against the stall's corner and said numbly, "You were spying on me."

"I wanted to learn the truth without frightening you. I wanted to get the books back, and I thought you'd deny having them if I demanded them outright. I wasn't even certain you had them. What else could I have done?"

"The honorable thing." Her voice broke. "Be honest."

"And what would you have done? Hand over a small fortune without a fight? Apologize for what your grandfather did almost fifty years ago? Tell me to take what's rightfully mine?" John grimaced with disgust. "Like hell."

"My grandfather didn't steal those books! They were given to him to take care of! After the war he couldn't find the owners. He tried for years!"

"Says who?"

"He left a letter for me when he died! He'd never told anyone about the books! He was afraid someone would accuse him of stealing them. Besides, he loved them. He spent years studying the diary and trying to learn more about Sir Miles. He left me all his notes. He didn't think of those books in terms of how much money they were worth!"

"Oh? Then why did he try to sell them last year?"

"What?"

"Last fall he wrote to a rare-book dealer in London. Told him about his 'gift' from an Englishman during the war. He asked about selling the books to a private collector."

Her shoulders sagged. "Is that how you found out about them?"

John smiled thinly and nodded. "Scotland Yard keeps records on stolen art objects and rare manuscripts. listed the books years ago, in case they ever showed up on the market. Dealers check those records to make certain they're not buying stolen property."

"So the dealer came to you and said he'd found out who had the books."

"That's right. I was tangled up in the little matter of defending myself from criminal charges at the time, or I'd have come here sooner. Be glad I went to prison. Otherwise, I'd have chased your beloved old grandpaps down. And I wouldn't have played nice."

"You'll wish you were fighting him instead of me, when I'm through with you. You'll wish you were back in prison." She spoke as if the words made her sick. "Nothing's too disgusting for you, is it? Taking bribes from terrorists. A shark has more conscience than you do."

"I was cheated out of my reputation, three months of my freedom, and my career with Scotland Yard," he told her, his voice soft and strained. "Everything that meant a damn to me. All because some people in high places knew I suspected their connections to a terrorist political group. To get me out of the way they set me up. I was 'framed,' as you Americans put it. I never took any bloody bribes. But you aren't going to believe that, either, are you?"

"No." She nearly spat the word. "There's not any reason for me to."

"We're at a standstill, then." He jerked at the chain. His eyes narrowed. "Take this thing off me."

She rose and left the stall without looking at him. Agnes heard the chain rattle as he leapt to his feet. Tall, handsome, nearly naked John Bartholomew, ex-Scotland Yard detective and consummate con artist, was chained to her barn wall. She intended to keep him that way.

"Agnes, you're not going to get anything out of this revenge," he called. His voice was calm, but rang with authority.

She ignored him and went out back to the water spigot. Agnes turned the water on full blast then dragged an armful of coiled hose down the barn's hallway. She stopped in front of the open stall door, shoved the floor fan aside with her bare foot, then angled her thumb over the hose's spout and plastered John with a long spray of cold water.

"I can't clean up your mind, but I can rinse off the rest," she told him sarcastically.

He stood still, because there wasn't much else to do, considering how short the chain was. John looked astonished and raised a hand only to shield his face when she aimed the spray at his head. His briefs turned into a translucent white skin over the bulge between his legs.

She prided herself on having the kindness not to aim at his crotch.

When he was soaking, with sheets of water running off him from head to foot, she carried the hose back outside and turned the water off. In the back of her mind she wondered what he'd do to her if he were freed at this moment.

Despite her fury, Aggie couldn't imagine him hurting her. She leaned against the side of the barn and, overcome by misery, covered her face. *Get real.*

When she returned to the stall he was naked. Giving her a black look, he tossed his rolled-up briefs at her. She was so startled that she let them smack her in the chest. They made a sopping wet trail as they slid down the front of her red shirt. She slapped them to the floor.

"If that's the way you want it," she told him, deliberately staring at his body. Anxiety, anger, and poignant memories made goosebumps on her skin. The man was never soft. Even now he mocked her with his arousal, or complimented her, if she continued to think like an idiot.

"A rabid dog doesn't need underwear," he said in a seething voice.

Aggie raised tearful eyes to his face. She'd admired

his body and his passion so much in the past few days. Now she had a hollow spot of despair inside her. "At least you're honest about some things."

"This won't work. You won't get anything out of me this way." He was losing his composure. He grabbed the chain between his hands and popped it. Muscles flexed violently in his arms. "Unlock this damned leash."

"Calm down. You'll be out of here and on your way back to England before you can say Buckingham Palace."

"Unlock the chain now," he said very slowly, emphasizing each word.

"Don't hold your breath."

She took Sassy out of her stall and put her back in the pasture with the other mares. Sassy had served her purpose in Aggie's plan. Distraught and exhausted, Aggie stumbled to the house, rummaged through her kitchen, and returned to the barn with a sack full of food. John was pacing as well as he was able in his tiny corner of the stall. Seeing him again was a fresh shock.

She had him chained to her barn wall. Naked. Really.

He halted and stared at her the way a panther suddenly notices its prey—his dark eyes narrowing, his stance tense as if he were preparing to leap.

Aggie tossed a clean milk jug filled with fresh water to him. He caught it, dropped it like a rock, and looked at the grocery sack with challenge. "Keep the damned food and water. I don't want it."

"My food and water has got to be better than what you were accustomed to in prison."

His silence was unnerving in its intensity. Setting the grocery bag on the floor, she pulled out a package of cookies, not looking at him. But his next words speared her with guilt. "You wouldn't joke about prison if you'd ever been there, Agnes. Especially if you knew you didn't deserve to be there."

Aggie kept her head down. She fought the constant

tightness in her throat. "I have an ex-husband in prison. I've got an idea what it must be like."

"The hell you do," he said, his voice becoming lethal. "The worst things you've ever had to face were humiliating articles about you and your husband in the newspapers, and parents who gambled away every penny you earned."

Her head shot up. "You looked up old articles about me?"

"Yeah. So I know the truth."

"You knew all along!"

Looking satisfied, he rubbed both hands up and down on his wet torso. "I wasn't considered one of the best detectives in London for nothing. I'm *very* thorough."

"You pretended that you didn't know!"

He crossed his arms over his chest and leaned against a wall, then propped one foot over the other. Even naked, with his sex lying against his thigh like a soldier who never stood at less than parade rest, he looked casual. "I assumed you'd tell me eventually. You trusted me. I deserve to be trusted, Agnes."

Aggie threw the bag of cookies at him. They bounced off his shoulder.

Surprise flashed across his face but he quickly subdued it. "Make you feel better?" he inquired.

"Not even close." She reached into the grocery bag then hurled a package of bologna at him. He intercepted it with one hand then tossed it aside.

But the overripe tomato she threw next caught him squarely in the stomach. He winced as the pulpy tomato pieces slid down his belly. The bulk of the tomato fell onto his sex and hung there precariously, then tumbled to the stall's bed of wood shavings.

Next Aggie threw a dripping slice of cold watermelon at him. Fierce with dignity, he stopped defending himself and, standing with his feet braced apart, endured the watermelon slice bouncing off his stomach. She followed it with an open cup of vanilla yogurt that splattered white goo on his chest, and finally a bag of pretzels that burst against his hard thighs.

"Enjoy your lunch," she told him curtly. "I'll be back around dark."

"You can't leave me here." He lunged forward, barely stopping before he choked himself. Only John Bartholomew could look anything but ridiculous covered in food stains. With a roguish beard shadow darkening his jaw, his dark wet hair tousled as if by the turbulence inside him, and his hazel eyes blazing challenge above a mouth set in granite, he hadn't been humiliated.

"Oh, can't I?" she countered. "Watch me."

"What are you after?" he asked in a soft, deadly voice. "I deserve your hatred for deceiving you, but not for who I am. Those books belong to me. Don't forget it."

"If it weren't for my grandfather, they'd have been lost in the war. So they're half mine!"

"Bloody hell! If that's what you expect me to agree to, give up."

"Before I found out the truth, I expected miracles from you. Congratulations. You had me believing that chivalry wasn't dead."

"You loved it. All that was left was for me to get a suit of chain mail and a white charger, and you might have loved *me*. But I was never Sir Miles of Norcross. I was just the modern stand-in, a man who played out your fantasy, and you wanted the fantasy."

Stunned, she shook her head weakly. Hadn't he seen how much she'd cared about *him*, even when he was brutally human, even that night he'd fought the muggers? "You don't really believe that. You're trying to make me feel guilty."

"Admit it, Agnes, you used me. You set impossible standards for the ideal man—the only man you were willing to trust. You couldn't find that man anywhere but in an ancient book. I was an acceptable substitute, but second best."

"Do you have any idea what Sir Miles wrote about in his diary?"

"No." He scowled. "Forget about that bloody fantasy and talk about your feelings for me. That's all I need to know!"

"My feelings for you?" Tears were creeping into her eyes. "You don't have any right to ask about them. You don't have any rights at all, at the moment." She went outside the stall, where she'd piled his clothes and shoes. Grabbing his khaki shorts and their belt, she went back and slung them at him. "There's a little of your dignity back. That's all you're gonna get from me."

"That's enough."

"Tonight I'm going to read you some of the words your ancestor wrote. I want to make sure you don't go back to England without hearing how an honorable man treats a woman."

"Lectures don't go well with captivity." He pointed at her warningly. "Take the chain off me, or you'll regret it."

"You can spend the whole afternoon thinking about tonight. Enjoy yourself."

"This plan of yours won't do a damned bit of good. I don't care what my glorious ancestor thought about honor and chivalry. He never had to deal with a red haired witch who chained men to barn walls. He's a fantasy built up in your imagination. I was never him."

She felt as if she were being torn apart. Every muscle in her body was clenched with control. Her voice quivering, she told him, "Two weeks ago I met the most gentle, caring, patient man I've ever known. He didn't come from my imagination and I didn't find him in a book. But you're right—he wasn't real. I'll never see him again. I'll look at you and think how much I miss him."

The fierce expression on John's face told her she'd

upset him more than she'd ever expected. "You can keep me chained up in your barn, Agnes. You can give me your lectures. You can try to humiliate me. I grant you that. But I'll make you think you've got a tiger on a leash by the time I'm through. If you're determined to believe I'm a bad man, I'll show you how bad."

"You only have a radius of about four feet to be bad in," she retorted, pointing at the chain. "So I'm not too worried."

His slow, slit-eyed smile almost unnerved her. "You'll worry," he promised.

John spent the long, hot afternoon sitting on the floor with his arms propped on updrawn knees and his head leaned back against the wall. Lost in anguished thought, he was only dimly aware of the chain dragging at his neck. Sweat snaked down his torso. He wadded the shorts up and used them as a pillow. If Agnes thought he was self-conscious about his body, she was wrong.

His legs and rump were plastered with wood shavings. He looked at himself, at his skin itchy with food residue despite the washing he'd done with the jug of water, at the shavings stuck in his body hair like large pieces of confetti. What Agnes had done made him furious. But more than ever he knew why he wanted her.

Only Agnes Hamilton would have had the sheer gall to do this to a man. He loved that outrageous part of her personality. He loved *her*, and knowing that he'd probably lost her forever made him want desperately to turn the calendar back two weeks and start over.

*Hello, I'm John Bartholomew, and I'm going to make you fall in love with* me, *just as I am—not a gentleman, but also not a liar. And the books be damned.*

But she wouldn't have wanted him then, would she?

He could have had any number of women who'd have been thrilled with him as he really was, but he'd had to pick the only one who wanted a reincarnated knight of the realm.

That hurt. He wouldn't let her see how much.

The late afternoon shadows made his pulse quicken. She'd be back soon, with her lectures and her pride. He had to shake up her attitude and make her admit that there'd been times, especially in bed, when she hadn't wanted a gentleman at all.

He picked up his long leather belt, looped it through the buckle, and began plotting.

# Nine

She hadn't expected him to be quiet and attentive. Was it possible he'd decided to listen, really listen? As Aggie hung an electric light and its extension cord in her corner of the stall she watched him from the corner of her eyes. Her stomach was in knots and every muscle in her body hummed with tension. Her eyes were grainy from crying all afternoon.

He was stretched out on his side, facing her, with his head propped on one hand. He'd cleaned himself up and put on his shorts. When she'd come into the stall after feeding the mares, he'd given her a thumbs-up and said gruffly, "Sexy outfit, Madame Warden."

Her floppy red sundress was faded and had a permanent horse-liniment stain on the skirt. She'd meant it to be comfortable, and she didn't think its loose, square bodice showed enough of her breasts to be considered sexy. While she sat down in the corner and tucked her bare feet under her, she kept eyeing John cautiously.

"Just shut up and listen," she ordered.

He raised a hand, palm up, as if inviting her to put chivalry in his grasp. Then he stretched his arm along his side and idly hung the hand over his hip.

*He's too relaxed*, a tormented little voice warned in

the back of her mind. But she wanted to believe he wanted to please her, that he felt a little sorry for using her to get close to the books.

Aggie set the stack of notebook pages in her lap and unclipped them. "Your ancestor loved his wife dearly," she began.

"The marriage was probably arranged by their parents or guardians. Most were, back then." John didn't sound belligerent, just factual.

Aggie flipped a page and read softly, "'I have never owed so great a debt as to your father, for sending you to me all those years ago, dear Eleanor. What had once been a duty to me was immediately a joy, the second I beheld you. And when I learned you felt the same, I thought my heart would burst with happiness.'"

John lifted his brows in a gesture of acceptance. "They were lucky. But what has this got to do with me?"

"He was wonderful to her. And she adored him. Listen." Aggie read, her voice trembling, "'And though my deceptions had you wondering if our marriage was nothing but a means to gain land and power, you know now that all my gentleness was no sham. I loved you from the start, though you didn't want to hear it, fearing it was a lie.'"

"You're saying Sir Miles wasn't as honorable as he seemed, eh?"

"No, I'm saying he never wanted to hurt Eleanor, no matter what the original reasons were for him wanting to marry her. From what he wrote, he had political reasons, at first. Eleanor's father was a Norman count with connections to the King of France. But Sir Miles fell in love with Eleanor, also."

"Are you saying I'm not like good old Sir Miles, because I wanted to hurt you? No. Never. You don't want to believe it, that's all."

Aggie turned more pages, searching her grandfather's translation through tear-filled eyes. "Why don't you stop making pointless remarks and simply listen?" She cleared her throat. "'I am doomed, sweet Eleanor. I am betrayed, and doomed. I will die here in this tower, without ever seeing you again. But keep our children safe and tell them that I love them, and you, and have them tell their children, and every generation after that, so every soul you and I create for centuries to come will know the power of our love."

John was silent, this time. She looked at him, her eyes burning. In the shadows his face was unreadable, but he was very still. "He died," she whispered. "But his and Eleanor's love didn't die. That's what's inside you. That's what I wanted you to know. You're carrying something precious inside you. You weren't meant to dishonor it."

"I haven't," John said in a low, emotional tone. "I came to get those books, but not to ruin your life."

"Oh, John," she said in despair, and covered her face with both hands. "Don't make excuses for what you wanted."

She dumped the note pages off her lap and stretched her feet out in front of her, her toes curled as if even they were drawn up in her misery. She bent over and cried softly into her hands.

"Agnes, don't. Please."

John's voice was throaty. She looked up, uncertain. He lay on his stomach, still facing her, his chin on the back of one hand. He held out a hand, palm up again, beckoning to her. She studied the distance between her toes and his hand. Nearly an arm's length separated them. He couldn't touch her, even if she wanted him to.

She moved a few inches to the right, not liking the confusion that churned in her. Crossing her feet at the ankles, she leaned back against the barn wall, wiped her face roughly, then reached for her grandfather's notes, to begin reading again.

John moved his outstretched hand so fast, it was only a flash on the edge of her vision. He jerked hard on something in the wood shavings. A loop of smooth leather caught Aggie's heels. In the same motion he snapped his hand forward, and the loop flipped over her feet. He jerked again, and it cinched tight around her ankles.

Everything happened in no more than two seconds.

Aggie screamed as he rose to his knees and threw his weight backward, with both hands wrapped around his end of the leather strap. His belt! she realized frantically. He'd made a loop of his belt, buried it in the wood shavings, and waited to catch her like a rabbit in a snare.

"Come here," he commanded in a growling tone. "Let's *really* talk."

He pulled her to him smoothly, despite her fierce wiggling and the way she dug the heels of her hands into the stall's bed as brakes. When he clamped both hands on her ankles she knew she couldn't escape.

While she yelled incoherently and tried to get her balance enough to sit up, he bound her feet with the belt and snugged it tightly. "Come *here*," he said again, with more authority.

Latching his hands under her knees, he dragged her protesting, writhing body into his corner as if he were a lion dragging a deer into his den. She finally managed to shove herself upright, but he caught her forearms and hoisted her off balance again. She lurched sideways in his powerful grip, and suddenly he had her pinned on her back.

Aggie hissed at him and struggled desperately, but above her his calm, dark eyes were set in an unyielding frown. He angled a long, hard leg over her twisting legs and lay down on top of her.

His weight effectively smothered her movements, though he wasn't hurting her, she realized in amazement, even with the hard grip of his hands on her wrists. With his face so near hers that she felt his breath on her mouth, he said in a low, steely voice, "If you really think I'm so bad, you ought to be afraid of me now."

"I'm not afraid of you," she retorted, her breasts straining against the pressure of his arms as she tried to catch her breath. "But that doesn't mean I'll ever trust you again."

"You'll trust me, Agnes. By God, you *will* admit that I'm not a criminal, at least."

He rolled her onto her stomach in one swift motion, as if he were flipping a log. When she dug her hands into the bedding and tried to scramble away he clamped one hand to her shoulder then sank the other into the back of her thin cotton sundress.

She gasped with shock when he ripped the material to her waist. "My dress!" she cried furiously. It wasn't that she cared about the dress, but she couldn't believe what he was doing.

"I'll buy you a new one," he said in a gritty voice.

Aggie tried to clench her arms to her chest, but he tugged the dress down to her elbows, then pried her arms down and jerked the dress to her hips. She wriggled forward as if she were a beached fish, but her movements only helped him work the dress down her legs and over her bound feet.

Rage filled her as she felt the balmy night air on her bare skin. She was wearing nothing but white cotton panties under the sundress.

"Now we're equally exposed," he told her. He clamped his hands around her waist and pulled her to him again. She twisted to face him and swung at him with one hand.

He grabbed her wrist, whipped his other arm around her so that her free arm was pinned by her side, and pressed her down on the bedding again. This time his naked torso was against her bare breasts. He wore only the shorts, and without the belt they hung so far down his belly that she could feel most of him against her outer hip.

When she drew her knees up and arched her back to fight him, he wrapped his leg over her again and hugged her into the curve of his body. She couldn't tell if he was aroused or not; she couldn't think clearly enough to notice. Aggie was practically spitting at him and making guttural fighting sounds in the back of her throat.

"Stop it," he ordered. "I want to talk, not growl at each other."

She glared up at him and grew silent, though she continued to flex and squirm. His mouth was a hard thin line, and his eyes were nearly black with emotion as they met hers. But now that she was so close, she saw something else in his gaze. Unmistakable sorrow.

"Do you think I'm capable of hurting you?" he asked. A muscle popped in his jaw. When she bit her lip and refused to answer, he shook her gently. "Agnes, you know I'm in control of you now. You know I can do anything I want to you. Do you think I would?" His hand tightened on her wrist. "Do you really think I'm capable of that?"

"No!" The word flew out of her before she realized she was going to say anything. It had a ragged, fervent sound. A sound of complete conviction.

She felt him tremble. His reaction quieted her as nothing else could. Stunned, she watched his expression soften a little. Was there relief in his eyes?

Aggie felt tears of confusion sliding down the sides of her face. "No," she repeated, her voice breaking. "I don't think you could hurt me in any *physical* way. I can't even picture it. There! Are you satisfied? That doesn't mean I trust you in any other way."

"Thank you for that, at least. Thank you." He shut his eyes and bowed his head over hers, almost touching his forehead to hers. She began to break apart inside, and chided herself for being such an easy mark. No apology of his would make up for what he'd done, the glib way he'd made her fall in love with him when all he'd wanted was to find out if she had Sir Miles's books.

When he looked at her again, his expression was stern. "I didn't intend to hide anything from you when I arrived here. I fell into a trap because I wanted to learn more about you. I couldn't have told you the truth and then expect to become your friend. Too much was at stake."

"Money," she retorted, her body stiffening with new anger. "You wanted to make sure nothing stood in the way of you getting those books, because they're valuable."

"Not just money." He clamped her tighter against him. When she gasped for breath he quickly pushed her hands over her head and trapped them against the wood shavings. Aggie inhaled gratefully with her arms no longer crunched atop her breasts. The only problem was, more of her bare torso was now intimately scrubbing against his chest.

"It's hard to be furious when we're this close," he said, watching her face. "Isn't it? Yes, Agnes, admit it. You aren't entirely convinced that I'm a monster."

She cursed, jackknifed under his leg, and tried to throw him off. But she only rammed her thighs against the hairy, unmovable weight of his leg. "Is this your idea of how to change my mind?" she asked grimly.

"At least this makes you remember how well we fit together."

"You didn't have to hold me down to keep me from leaving. That's what I remember. Not like now. That's the difference."

"The difference between my idea of romance and what you *think* I enjoy? You're wrong if you think I don't care whether you hate me. It tortures me to hold you like this, knowing that not one ounce of your body wants to be under me. It's torture to feel your nipples against me and know that I can't kiss them, or feel those dangerous legs of yours struggling to get free and kick the hell out of me. I'd rather you part your thighs oh-so-sweetly and ask me to put my hand between them, then ask me to put a much more interesting part of my body in my hand's place."

"Stop it!"

He smiled thinly. "When I think of how you felt about me this time yesterday, I want to beat my head against a wall. Remember? Before you left for work at the pub, you insisted that I make love to you in the shower. And then again in bed. And you were crying with pleasure before we finished. Only about twenty-four hours ago, Agnes. Can I be such a different, undesirable man today?"

His provocative words made her quiver. Her voice breaking, she said, "Did I make it easy for you? Was I so desperate that you thought I was funny?"

"Agnes, *no*. Don't you see? Everything that happened between us was real, and beautiful. I tried not to lie to you about who I was. I tried very hard to be vague when you asked questions, but you were so damned determined to see a hero instead of a man."

"I saw *both*," she replied through clenched teeth.

"Because you thought I was wealthy and aristocratic."

"Because you were loving and decent!"

"And wealthy and aristocratic."

Aggie made a guttural sound of frustration and tried to pull her arms out of his restraining grip. But he only clamped his hands onto hers and wound his fingers through hers. "That's cozier," he said with a hint of sarcasm.

Aggie jerked on his hands but stopped when she realized how much her movements made her breasts jiggle against his chest. "Why couldn't you have told me the truth about your background?" she demanded.

"Even if you didn't tell me you were here to get your ancestor's books back!"

"You'd have turned me out in a second if I'd said I was ex-Scotland Yard and had spent time in prison."

Aggie stared at him with grim dismay. "I'm not a snob! Do you think I go around judging people that way? Me? With the kind of background *I* have? I'm the last person in the world who'd condemn you for having a bad reputation."

"So you're willing to believe that I'm innocent of the bribery charge?"

"I don't know." Hope and anger were written on his face in harsh lines. His dark eyes were narrowed as if he'd built a shield around himself and left only that pair of vulnerable spots to let pain in and out.

"You judged me *hard*, Agnes," he said in a low voice. "As soon as you heard the basics about me from Detective Herberts, you made up your mind, and you don't want to change it. So how can you say you wouldn't have judged me wrongly from the first?"

"But you *didn't* tell me the truth about yourself. I had to hear it from a stranger."

"Does that make such a terrible difference?"

"Yes!"

"No." His hands tightened on hers. A sinew flexed in his throat as he swallowed harshly. Aggie felt as if he and she shared every emotion, even the hidden ones neither wanted to reveal. Their straining bodies and the night's warm, pungent air made a primitive scent.

To Aggie it was a reminder of the potent sexual mood between her and John during the past week. How could she have been wrong about a man who was so lusty and yet incredibly unselfish in bed?

"You didn't want an ordinary man," he insisted, leaning over her. Even more of his body pressed against her, and every inch of him was asking her to accept his explanation.

Aggie searched his eyes. "I never considered you ordinary!"

"Because you loved the lies I told you about myself."

"I loved the way you treated me! What woman doesn't love hearing that she's special? I believed you meant it! That's what hurts the most—that you lied about your *feelings* for me."

"I wasn't lying."

She exploded with rage, twisting violently under him. "You can have the books! But don't try to make a fool of me anymore!"

"Is this a lie?" He kissed her gently and quickly, brushing his lips over hers.

Aggie cried out in anger and surprise, turning her face away. Tension hummed inside her for a new reason. His kiss made her madder, but not afraid or disgusted. He still had the power to make her want him.

She shut her eyes and cursed bitterly. Aggie sensed him watching her, his face so close she felt the warmth from it and heard the harsh rhythm of his breath, matching hers.

"If you insist, keep believing I misled you about my past," he whispered. His hands sank deeper into hers, and his thumbs stroked the tender skin along the sides of her palms. "But don't you *dare* think I didn't want you more than I've ever wanted a woman before in my life. I told you from the beginning how fantastic you were, and I meant it. I still do."

"*No.*" She shook her head fiercely, and new tears drowned her eyes. She blinked rapidly and swallowed the embarrassing sobs that rose in her throat. "I heard what I wanted to hear and thought you had no reason to make any of it up. But you had *plenty* of reasons."

He brushed another devastatingly soft kiss across her forehead. "If you think I'm known for chasing and seducing women with my quotes from Greek philosophy, you're *very* wrong. In fact, women have always chased *me*, so all I usually have to do is wait."

He touched his lips to her wet cheeks. "I'm not used to charming a determined loner like you. You see? I couldn't plan a devious attack on you with my skills as an upper-class Casanova. I had to rely on the truth. I told you how I really felt about you. And I *showed* you, something I'm much more skilled at."

As if to prove his point, he sank his mouth onto hers. Aggie inhaled sharply and murmured a word onto his parted lips. But the word was garbled, even in her own mind, and it came out more as a sound of confusion than a denial.

She refused to move her lips in response to his, but he continued kissing her anyway, lightly tugging at her mouth and angling his head to tantalize her from new directions. Each time he pulled back a little then came down on her mouth with a different mood—tender, angry, seductive, sweet.

"Here's the truth," he said gruffly. Her hands had relaxed; he kept his hands on top of them but loosened his grip and slid his fingers down to her palms. He stroked lightly with his fingertips while he never stopped kissing her. In a distracted part of her mind Aggie realized that her hands had uncurled and were enjoying his caress.

"I'm not a criminal," he whispered, the words feathering her mouth. "And you can trust me as much now as before. Completely." He held Aggie's attention with the hypnotic sincerity in his eyes. "When we made love, you saw a very real and very vulnerable man, not a man who was planning every word and action."

He rose on his elbows and drew his hands down her arms, trailing his fingers on the soft undersides, which lay exposed to him the same as her emotions were. He framed her face, and his thumbs smoothed tears from the tender skin under her swollen eyes.

Aggie looked up at him in a daze. This was the John Bartholomew who'd won her love, the man whose voice and touch made her drunk with desire, the man who was capable of the most uninhibited passions but also heart-melting tenderness.

Could he be the kind of man who'd have done everything to deceive her into telling him about the medieval books?

She didn't know. Her thoughts were jumbled. But one thing was disturbingly clear: The man was proving that he could trap her the way she'd trapped him—but he didn't need a chain.

A chill ran through her. If she didn't stop indulging these crazy fantasies, she'd lose the rest of her dignity to John's smooth seduction. She formed a cold smile and stared hard into his eyes. "I don't want you. I want the man I met two weeks ago. There's no comparison. So why don't you let me go and we'll get this over with?"

At first he looked stunned. Then a hard, carefully concealing expression came over his face. "That man was as much a ghost as your beloved Sir Miles. But it wasn't a ghost who made you happy. It wasn't a ghost you were begging for more every night."

Suddenly he straddled her, planting his knees on either side of her. Aggie's heart raced as she stared at the overwhelmingly, potently masculine image he made. The chain draped from his neck to one shoulder and then curled gracefully down one side of his chest, as if it were part of some barbaric warrior's insignia.

He stroked a hand down her body. "I'm a warm, eager flesh-and-blood man, Agnes. That's what you needed. A man who loved making you smile, in bed and out. A man who *still* wants to make you smile."

"A man who even asked me to marry him," she replied in an icy tone. "How far would you have gone to get the books?"

"You laughed at the proposal. You were terrified. You'd never have said yes."

"Terrified?" she echoed. "What makes you think that?"

"It threatened you. Too much reality." His gaze moved down her body. "You'd rather give yourself to me in ways that seemed much safer to you."

Aggie resisted an urge to cover her breasts. She felt sad and vulnerable, and needing him upset her. She casually rose to her elbows and tried to ignore her nakedness. When she glanced down she saw the pattern of his chest hair on her right breast, where he'd lain against her so tightly.

"I don't have any trouble making commitments," she told John. Small shivers of misery and undeniable sexual tension made her ache inside. "I'm the one who was married once, not you."

"You weren't married," he argued bluntly. "You were playing at it, playing a game you couldn't win, because you didn't know what kind of man you really needed."

He leaned forward and planted a hand on either side of her hips. Abruptly she was confronted by his nearness again. His brutally handsome face and fierce mood were posed a breathless fraction from her face. She had to tilt her head all the way back to look directly at him. Her throat felt exposed, and as his gaze rested on it she thought, with an internal quiver of arousal, that he could easily bend his head and sink his teeth into her. Her awkward position made her breasts thrust upward, as if offering themselves to him against her will.

"I don't need *you*," she said. But the tautness of her neck compressed her voice and made it sound hoarse, even seductive.

His eyes glittered. "I dare you to prove that." He scooped both arms around her waist and pulled her up to him. She hung in his embrace, her hands reaching automatically for a grip on his shoulders. He coupled her to him with his mouth, possessive and demanding this time, making her moan deep in her throat, a sound of defeat.

She moved her lips against his, then caught his lower lip between her teeth and bit him hard. He jerked away but immediately kissed her again, coaxing her with sensual shoving motions of his jaw until her lips parted and he slipped his tongue inside.

She trembled with anger, grief, and excitement. No other man in the world could have caught her in this spell. She wanted to fight him at the same time she wanted everything to be perfect again. It never could be, she thought wretchedly. Why was she torturing herself this way?

John bent farther over her as she kissed him. He closed his arms tighter around her, then raised one hand to the back of her head. He sank his fingers into her tangled hair and pulled her head back. With his eyes burning into hers he said gruffly, "I'm not that fantasy you wanted, but I'll never deliberately hurt or disappoint you. I think you know it."

"The books," she said numbly. "You only want the books."

"I want you *and* the books."

"What are you going to do with them?"

"Sell them, the same as you would have done."

"No!" Aggie returned to earth with a jolt. Her grip on his shoulders became a hard shoving motion as she tried to push herself away. "Let me go!"

His expression became grim but he released her. She scooted back from him, trying to draw her legs from between his. But he wasn't about to let her get away completely. He grabbed her bound ankles and sat back on the bedding. Lifting her feet into his lap, he wound a fist into the leather belt and held firmly.

"You were going to sell those books eventually," he insisted, but he looked at her with a puzzled frown.

"No, I want to protect them, the same way my grand-father did!"

"Dammit, Agnes, why don't you admit he was going to sell them? The only reason he didn't was because he got nervous when the broker in London backed out."

"He could have sold those books years ago, if the money was all he cared about! In the letter he left to me he explained why he never tried. Your grandparents trusted him to take care of the books. After the war he couldn't find them, then when he learned they'd died, he tried to find their daughter. But it was impossible to track down an orphan in a country where there were so many orphans and so few records of what happened to them"

"Maybe what you're saying is true. Maybe he didn't steal the books. But right before he died he *was* planning to sell them."

"He wanted me to have plenty of money for this ranch. He only wanted to sell the books for my sake. In his letter he told me to sell them if I had to, but to read his translation of the diary, first."

She shook her head. "I saw why he felt so protective of what Sir Miles had written. The diary may be valuable to collectors because it's rare and ancient, but it's valuable to me because it shows that there really are people who never stop loving each other and never let the world take away their dignity." She was crying now. "That's why I don't think I could have made myself sell it."

"I'll tell you what helps a person keep the *dignity* you love so much," John said softly, his voice strained. "Having the money to tell the rest of the world to take a flying leap."

Aggie braced her hands behind her and gritted her teeth. With her feet trapped in his lap she once again felt like a rabbit caught in a snare. All she could do was sit there, naked except for her panties, and glare at John in helpless rage, while tears slid down her face. "You're going to sell the diary and prayer book," she said flatly. "I can see it on your face. You're not even going to read the diary's translation. You're just going to hand the books over to some rare-books dealer and rake in your money."

He nodded curtly. "Do you have any idea how much the books are worth?"

"No."

"Probably a million pounds, to a private collector. That's over a million-and-a-half American dollars, Agnes. Is sentiment worth ignoring that much money?"

"It doesn't matter what I think, or what I want. They're your books. I won't fight you for them. *My* dignity is worth too much to me. It's about all I have left, and I'm going to hang on to it."

"We'll see how you feel about my decision when I'm rich. Think of it, Agnes. I'll be that wealthy man you wanted me to be."

"You'll never understand what I wanted you to be. But it didn't have anything to do with money."

His eyes were black with frustration. He started to say something, but the dogs began to bark outside the barn. Within seconds Aggie heard a car's tires on the driveway's crushed shell and gravel. She gasped.

"Expecting a visitor?" John asked calmly.

"No, but whoever it is might come in here looking for me!"

He clamped his hands tighter around her ankles. "If I can't leave this stall, you can't leave."

"For godsakes, John, I didn't bring the padlock key in here with me!" Let me go, and I'll get it, I swear!"

He chuckled darkly. "An oath easily made is easily broken. No, if I have to sit here chained to the wall, you can damn well stay with me."

She heard the car come to a stop in the yard. Aggie looked down at her nakedness frantically. John tugged on her feet. "I'm such a gentleman that I'll *allow* you to crawl over and get your sundress." But he didn't turn her feet loose. "Go ahead," he urged, as she scowled at him. "You can wiggle."

She cursed under her breath, rolled over onto her stomach, and squirmed to within arm's reach of the dress, which he'd tossed across the stall. Grabbing it, she sat up and slipped it over her head. Wood shavings itched on her skin and clung maddeningly to her hair, and the dress's torn back gaped open, but at least she was covered.

John slid back into his corner and pulled her across the soft bedding. "Come along, my little red-haired hamster," he said with a calm smile.

"Let me go!"

"I let you get your dress. That's as far as my nobility will stretch. Now come here and do what I say, if you want to salvage your precious dignity."

They heard the car door open and shut. Aggie gave in and scooted over to him. He leaned against the stall's back wall, draped the chain out of sight down his back, then he took her arm and pulled her to his side. She tucked her belted feet under the dress's skirt.

She heard the visitor walking in the graveled yard. The footsteps faded in the direction of her house. John put an arm around her, crossed his legs in front of him, then drew one of her arms around the front of his neck. "There," he said glibly. "If you keep your arm still, no one can see my chain. You won't be forced to explain your bizarre technique for capturing men."

When she stared at him in seething anger, he smiled and began flicking wood shavings off his rumpled shorts. "Our visitor will think we're just a rambunctious pair of lovers."

"You like to humiliate me?"

"No. In case you've forgotten, I'm the one who's chained to the wall. I'm the one who stands to be humiliated."

"You don't look humiliated at all."

"I'm more concerned with what's happening between you and me than about what some visitor thinks about this situation."

They stopped talking as the footsteps came crunching back across the yard and approached the barn. Aggie found herself gripping John's neck harder and inching a little closer to him. Deep down she admitted that he made her feel safe even now.

"Hello?" an unfamiliar male voice called from the barn's open door.

"Come right in," John answered cheerfully.

Aggie pinched the back of his neck in revenge.

The man who came to the stall door and gaped at them was small, slender, and dressed in gaudy yellow trousers and a bright orange, short-sleeved shirt. A large turquoise pin was fastened at the center of the shirt's buttoned collar, and a matching watch swallowed his wrist. With his blond hair pulled back in a ponytail he was very West Coast, reminding Aggie of the cocky, tasteless young TV executives she'd known in California.

"Hello," she said calmly. "Are you looking for someone in particular?"

He was still staring at her and John. Finally he got his wits together and shifted his attention to her alone. From the familiarity in his gaze she assumed he remembered her from TV. Occasionally people recognized her, or knew vaguely that they'd seen her somewhere before. "You don't know me, Aggie, but I know you," he said with a big, bright smile that worried her. "My name's Allen Harper. I thought I'd look you up in person. I flew in from L.A. this afternoon. Uh, can we talk in private? Looks like I caught you at a bad time, but I think you really want to hear what I've got to say."

"Certainly," John interjected. "Go ahead."

Aggie's stomach twisted with a premonition of troule. She'd had all the trouble she could stand for one lifetime, tonight. "This isn't a good time."

"You did some work with my dad," Allen Harper continued, as if he really didn't care whether she wanted to talk or not. "Billy Harper. Does the name ring a bell? He was a photographer."

She nodded vaguely, her nerves ready to snap. "Yeah. He did the publicity shots for a movie I was—" The rest of the sentence froze in her throat. John seemed to sense her distress, because his arm tightened around her.

"My dad died last year," Allan Harper went on pleasantly, his eyes narrowing as he studied her reaction. "I'm a photographer too. Sort of inherited his business, I guess you could say. I want to talk to you about the photos you did with him."

"Go ahead, talk," John urged smoothly.

Aggie felt the blood pooling in her stomach. She knew *exactly* what sleazy little Allen Harper wanted. The day's events crashed down on her, and she felt as if her shoulders would break from the weight. John had betrayed her, and now her past had betrayed her too.

"Excuse me, I'd better go talk to Mr. Harper alone," she said to John, without victory in her voice, even though she'd found a smooth way to get out of his clutches.

"I'll wait outside," Harper said cheerfully, and left.

John took her shoulders and turned her to face him. "What does he want?"

"None of your business. And if you don't let me go, I'll scream. If I'm not mistaken, Allen Harper is so sleazy he'll call the police just to see some excitement."

"Are you in some kind of trouble?"

"No."

"You're not telling the truth."

"I guess it's a habit I picked up from you."

"*Stop it.*" He shook her gently. "Tell me what he wa
hinting about."

"Are you going to let me go, or am I going to scream
I swear, I don't have anything left to lose, so don't pus'
me."

He studied her leaden expression for a moment, the
slowly released her. As he pulled her feet forward an
untied them he told her, "Whatever's wrong, I want t
help you."

"I don't want your help. I want you out of my life."

"It's not that easy."

"Yes it is."

She rose, grabbed one of the blankets he'd bee
sitting on during the day, and wrapped it around h
shoulders to hide the dress's torn back. Bits of woo
shavings fell out of her tangled hair. She knew her fa
was red and swollen, and her bare feet were dirty.

She decided that she looked much, much better tha
she felt.


John listened as Harper drove away, after talking wi
Agnes for a long time. Every minute of their secr
conversation tore at him. Harper had something on he
probably something to do with his old man's phot
graphs. What had Agnes done, posed for some nu
shots six years ago when she was so confused an
desperate?

Good lord, a few nudie photos didn't matter. Some
the most respectable newspapers in London print
huge color photos of naked models. Nobody thoug
anything of it. He frowned, recalling Agnes's hard wo
to change her life, and the way she fought for her pri
She wouldn't consider naked photos of herself son
thing to shrug off.

In fact she'd be terribly humiliated if that sleazy lit
pastel-colored con man had found an old file of phot

and was looking for ways to cash in on them. Some tabloid or men's magazine could grab a few extra readers with her photos and a headline such as "Former Child Star Bares All," or something equally stupid.

John got up and looked out the stall's window, clenching the sill angrily when Harper left and Agnes walked into her house. She came out a few minutes later, wearing a different sundress and sneakers. She carried a suitcase.

John watched in stunned disbelief as she got into her truck and left.

Eventually a huge, hulking blond-haired man arrived. "I'm Oscar Rattinelli," he told John with a lethal edge in his voice. "And since Aggie made me swear not to hurt you, you're in luck." He tossed John a tiny silver key.

"Where is she?" John asked anxiously as he unlocked the chain from his neck and slung it aside.

"She said for you to get the medieval books then get off her place. I'm gonna stay here until you do that, and then I'm gonna follow you to the airport and watch you get on a plane."

"I'm not going. Frankly, I suspect you're big enough to drag me out of here, but that's a chance I'll take. I want to see Agnes. Where is she?"

"I'd love to crack a few of your bones, but there's no point. Agnes won't be back anytime soon, so waiting here won't do you any good. I'm gonna take care of things here for a few days. She won't come back until you're gone for good. So take the books and get out of her life."

John cursed bitterly. He had no choice but to go. "I'll take the books, but tell her I'll be back to explain."

"Right. She'll believe *that*."

John grabbed the sheaf of notes she'd left on the stall's floor. He wanted to read the diary's translation, if only because it would make her happy. But reading would have to wait. For now he had a long trip to England ahead of him, and an eight-hundred-year-old legacy to claim.

---

alfred Dolbrook was short, stout, and as determined
s a bulldog. His pin-striped suit, derby hat, and bow tie
ere so proper they would have made Aggie smile
rdinarily, but in the week since John had left she'd felt
nat all the laughter had been drained out of her.

Agnes wished it were later in the evening so the bar
ould be crowded. Oscar had nothing better to do than
tare at Dolbrook while he shoved clean beer glasses
nto a shelf. Oscar had seen how tormented she'd been
n the past week by John's actions and Allen Harper's
sit, and Oscar was ready to tear someone apart.

She leaned over the Conquistador's bar between cus-
mers and shook her head at Dolbrook again. "I can't
elp you find John," she repeated. "I don't know where
e was going after he went back to England. I'm sur-
rised you could track him here. Is he in trouble again?"

Dolbrook stared at her. His eyes twinkled over a
ignacious nose. "The bloody hellion is *always* in
ouble."

She tried not to show her despair. "I guess you're not
friend of John's."

"Me, miss? A friend of *his*?" Dolbrook cackled. "I hope
e day never comes when I'm reduced to being friends

with a man who never listens to an order and neve plays by the department's rules."

"You worked with him at Scotland Yard?"

"For too many years." Dolbrook bowed slightly. "*In spector* Dolbrook, at your service."

She fought the tears in her eyes, but Dolbrook peere at her closely and saw them. "I think we'd better have talk in private about John Bartholomew."

Oscar jerked a thumb toward the hall that led to hi office. "You upset Aggie and I'll break your pound not into shillings."

"How charming to meet you," Dolbrook said cheerful as he followed Aggie to the back.

After she shut the door to Oscar's tiny office sh pivoted toward the inspector anxiously. "Did John real take bribes from terrorist groups?"

Dolbrook arched a bushy black brow. "John tak bribes? Did I say he was a criminal? No, I only said h was a hellion."

"You mean he really was framed? He's innocent?"

Dolbrook nodded. His upper lip curled in disgust. "H was framed. John may be a hellion *and* a rebel, but ne: to me he's the best and most honest detective at th Yard."

Aggie sat down limply in a chair. "I didn't belie him."

Dolbrook perched his stocky but dapper body on corner of Oscar's desk. He idly brushed lint from th derby, which he held carefully in both hands. "Don't fe bad, miss. He's not an easy man to get to know. He gre up hard, and he keeps to himself."

"Why are you looking for him?"

Dolbrook's eyes were proud as they met hers. "To t him he's been cleared. The conviction's going to overturned. He can even come back to his career at th Yard."

"That's wonderful." But she was crying silently, and not from joy.

"Here, now, what's the matter? I think you better explain what happened between you and John."

She told him how they'd met, and about the books, and how John had deceived her. Dolbrook listened intently, his brows raised in perpetual curiosity, as if he'd never heard a stranger story in his life. "He got close to me just to find out about the books," Aggie finished, scrubbing tears away with the tail of her bar apron.

Dolbrook patted her shoulder. "I told you John never plays by the rules, but I also told you he's honest. He doesn't cheat people. But maybe I better tell how he grew up. Then you can understand him a little better."

Now it was her turn to listen in rapt silence as the detective revealed John's ugly boyhood with a pathetically shy mother, who'd died when he was young, and a disreputable father who'd been addicted to gambling.

*Addicted to gambling, just like my parents,* she thought numbly.

Dolbrook told her how John grew up surrounded by the snobbery of upper-class England and the shame of his own ruined heritage. It would have made any man hard and cynical. It would have made most turn out badly. But John had worked his way up. He'd had to become tough, to do it.

"He thought I wanted the pampered businessman he pretended to be," she told Dolbrook wearily. "But that wasn't true. I wish he could believe I respect him. He has his own brand of nobility."

"That's hard for him, miss. He's seen a lot of hypocrisy, and he's known some so-called 'noble men' who stabbed him in the back."

Aggie huddled in the chair and buried her face in her hands. "I'm glad you told me all this. I never had a chance to learn about the real John Bartholomew. I wish I had known the truth earlier. It's too late now."

"Why?"

"I love him, but I don't think he'll ever forgive me for some of the things I said and did to him. And I don't know if he wants the kind of love I have to offer."

"I think you're wrong, miss. I think he's been waiting all his life to find the right woman. I suspect you're her."

Aggie shook her head and looked up at Calfred Dolbrook leadenly. "This isn't a medieval fable. John's not coming back to fight any dragons or pledge his undying love. He's not sentimental."

Dolbrook stood and sighed sadly. "If he shows up again, you tell him to call me at the Yard."

She nodded to be polite, while deep inside she was withering from the certainty that John would never come back.


The next night, not long before closing time, Allen Harper sauntered in. Pure disgust rose in Aggie's throat along with dread. It was a good thing Oscar was in his office going over the books. It was a good thing she didn't have a baseball bat.

"You flew out from L.A. again just to see me?" she asked Harper, as he settled his slender rump on a bar stool. "You're wasting your time. I haven't got twenty five thousand dollars. I told you that. I can take the embarrassment. Go ahead and sell the pictures to some trash magazine."

"I'm not here to see *you*," Harper said with a puzzled smirk. "You don't know why I'm here?"

"Why should I know?"

"Well, well, I won't spoil the surprise. How about fixing me a martini?"

"Because this bar has a minimum-sleaze require ment, and you don't make the grade."

Allen leaned toward her, tossed a slender briefcase on the bar, and propped his chin in his hands. Once again he was dressed in pastels, with thick gold-and-gemstone jewelry at his throat and on his wrist. His blond ponytail swayed gently in the breeze from an overhead fan.

He studied her through slitted eyes. "You know, if you'd be willing to do a new photo session, with me in charge this time, we could both make some money off that perfectly stacked package of yours."

"Your dad had class. You'll go a lot farther in the business if you at least pretend to have the same kind of morals he had."

"He was a soft touch. Too soft, because he didn't hold his clients to their legal responsibilities."

"When he saw that they'd made a mistake and wanted to change it? No, he was too 'soft' to hold them to the legalities of a piece of paper they'd signed when they were desperate. I knew he could sell my pictures anytime he wanted to, since I'd signed a release, but I also knew he wouldn't sell them if I asked him not to."

"Well, sweetcakes, it's too bad you were squeamish about showing off that wonderful pair of friends you've got on your chest. But I'm going to make some money off them, and it's completely legal."

Harper smiled at her again and leaned farther over the bar, staring at her chest in the loose white pullover she wore with pink shorts. Aggie turned her back and began violently polishing highball glasses. "I don't know why you're here or what your game is, but I'm giving you five minutes to leave before I wrap a bar towel around your throat and make your eyeballs pop."

"I love the little beauty mark between your breasts," Harper said coyly. "God, I wish you hadn't been so silly about full nudity. I'm dying to know if you're a redhead all over."

Aggie heard him make a strangled sound, like a

squawk. "I can make certain you die," a deep British voice said.

She whirled around and met John's dark eyes. He had a hand around the back of Harper's neck, and the much smaller man was hunched over the bar as if he knew his vertebrae were in danger of being snapped. John's face was stern, but a hint of humor curled one corner of his mouth up as he pulled Harper back and set him firmly on the bar stool.

When he released the nape of Harper's neck, Harper coughed nervously and smiled at him. "Glad you're on time."

Stunned, Aggie could barely make sense of what was happening. "What are you doing here?" she asked John. "You have a meeting with *him*?" She jerked her head toward Harper.

John nodded as he smoothed a hand down a beautiful white suit that looked new and very expensive. A gold pin gleamed at the throat of his pale gray shirt. It was set with a large onyx that added another dark accent to his hair and eyes.

He looked like a man who'd recently acquired a fortune. Her heart sank when she thought of the books.

He turned his attention to Harper. "Hand them over."

"Your wish is my command." Harper opened his briefcase, took out a thick manila envelope and laid it on the bar.

Aggie stared in bewilderment as John handed it to her. "Take a look through the negatives and see if you think everything's there."

Her hands shaking, she ripped open the envelope, turned her back, and numbly studied a handful of color negatives against the bright light of a neon beer sign. "I think so," she said weakly, shoving the negatives back into the envelope as she turned around again.

"Good." John pulled a piece of paper from an inner

pocket in his jacket and handed it to Harper. "A money order for the whole amount. Just as you wanted."

"Perfect. I'm so happy to make a deal that protects Aggie's privacy."

At that moment, Oscar stalked out of his office. When he saw John his face took on an expression like an enraged gorilla's. "What are you doing here?"

To distract him, Aggie pointed fiendishly to Harper. "Guess who this is! The man who wants to sell nude photos of me."

Oscar grunted, and his face turned livid. Harper quickly began tucking his money order into his pink jacket. John clamped a hand on his wrist. "Put it in your briefcase."

Harper had the good sense to do that without asking why. He snapped the case shut and stared at John fearfully. "Why?"

"I wouldn't want it to get wet." John sank both hands into the back of Harper's jacket and hauled him out of the bar.

Aggie ran after them, with Oscar right behind her. She arrived on the porch that overhung the bay in time to see John toss Harper into the murky surf ten feet below. Harper splashed like a drenched pink flamingo. Big waves washed him toward shore.

"He was too small to hit," John explained in an utterly serious voice. "But I had to make my point *some* way."

"Maybe I misjudged you," Oscar said to John. He sounded astonished and cheerful. He poked Aggie's shoulder. "Maybe you misjudged John." Then he went back inside, leaving the two of them alone in the darkness.

John faced her. "We need to talk."

"Inspector Dolbrook was here yesterday looking for you."

"I know. His message caught up with me in London."

They were silent. She felt as if a thousand invisible

strings were trying to pull words out of her, but she was afraid she'd say something he didn't want to hear. She was in shock. He held out a hand. "Let's take a walk on the beach." He hesitated. His voice was gruff. "If you wish, my lady?"

Her knees went soft and she put her hand in his quickly. Seconds later he was pulling her along at a run down the narrow wooden walkway that led to the bayfront street. Waiting there was a gleaming black Mercedes sports coupe with the top down.

He picked her up and set her in the passenger seat, then climbed into the driver's side. Aggie took her bar apron off and clutched it in her lap as they sped down the bayfront boulevard and left the shops and street lamps of town behind. They crossed the Bridge of Lions in the light of a half-moon and headed toward the beach a few miles away.

She couldn't talk to John with the wind roaring over them, and she was glad. The car, his suit, the money he'd given Harper—yes, he'd sold the books. She thought about the diary and grieved as if she'd lost a dear friend, but then she looked at John and felt a surge of elation.

He had his family inheritance now. Maybe he'd believe that she didn't care about the money, and they could get on with their lives. Their life together? But he had his job back at Scotland Yard, the job he loved. Maybe he'd only come here to smooth things over and say his apologies before he went home again.

By the time he slid the Mercedes into a sandy spot along the beach road, she was subdued and worried. He vaulted out, came to her side, and lifted her over the door effortlessly. "Buy a car with doors that open, next time," she told him.

"It's rented."

"Oh. Oh! Of course. You wouldn't buy a car in America when you're going back to England soon."

"I wouldn't buy a Mercedes, period. I can't afford it."

Before she could ask a stunned question, he grabbed her hand and tugged her swiftly toward the dunes between the road and the beach. "But you sold the books!" she said, trying to keep her footing in the deep sand. "Didn't you? You look like you did!"

John led her between hills of sand higher than their heads. "I look rich because I'm wearing a nice suit? I want you to know something, Agnes. This is the second white suit I've bought in your honor, and I'm not going to buy any more. I feel like an ice-cream salesman."

"In my honor?" she repeated, puzzled.

They were deep within the dunes, now. "White knight, and all that rot," he muttered.

"Oh!"

He halted her when they reached a very private little valley surrounded by dunes and tall sea oats. John faced her and took her other hand. "Yes, I sold the books. But I'm not any better off than I was before. Not in terms of money, at least."

"But you said they were worth a million pounds."

"To a private collector. But instead I sold them to a little museum that specializes in medieval history. They'll be studied, and cherished, and preserved, and anytime either of us wants to see them, they'll be available."

Aggie swayed with astonishment. "Why did you change your mind?"

"Don't you think I'm capable of putting honor above money?"

She stared at him in silence, fighting the knot of tears in her throat, then lifted his hands and kissed each one. She laid her cheek against them and said brokenly, "Sir John, I think you're capable of all sorts of wonderful things."

"I read the diary," he said gruffly. "The translation, that is. It was magnificent, just as you said."

"And that made you change your mind?"

"No." When she raised her head to look at him, he

kissed her. "I'd already made up my mind to sell the books to the museum."

She smiled in adoration. "I'm sorry I ever doubted you."

"Well, I certainly didn't make it easy to believe in me. I thought I needed a fortune so I could fit the image you loved."

She shook her head gently. "I still wish you hadn't sold the books. I don't care about the money. I don't care about some fairy-tale, Camelot image."

"I'm glad you don't mind about the money, Agnes, because a modest little museum can't pay much for rare books."

"I think you placed them where they'll be loved, and that's important. I *don't care* about the money. I swear."

"Good, because it's all gone. In American currency, it was only about twenty-five thousand. I gave it to Allen Harper."

She gasped. "You did that for *me*? You gave up every penny of your inheritance?"

He pulled her to him. "Consider it an act of gallantry," he whispered. "As true and heartfelt as anything my ancestor could have done in my place."

She gripped his jacket lapels. "Be *yourself* for me! I loved Sir Miles for the way he loved Eleanor. But I love you for the way you love me!" She halted, hating the words she'd blurted out without thinking. "I shouldn't have put it like that," she amended quickly, her voice hoarse and apologetic. "I don't know if you love me or not."

He lifted her off her feet and looked closely into her shadowed face. "You love me? God, Agnes, do you really?"

"Yes! I love you for so *many* reasons. And none of them have to do with your ancestors, or your parents, or who you said you were when you wanted me to believe the best about you. I *know* the best about you, and you *are* that gentle, patient, understanding man I fell in love with."

She put her arms around his neck and kissed him wildly. He made a gruff sound of happiness against her mouth. "I fell in love with you the night we met."

He pulled her legs out from under her, scooped her into his arms, then knelt and lowered her to the sand. She circled his neck and drew him down with her. They kissed slowly.

"You need a partner for your ranch," he told her. He removed his jacket and spread it like a blanket.

She trembled and tried to keep her voice steady. "Have any suggestions?"

"Oh, yes. Someone who loves horses, knows how to mend fences, and can help you make enough money to keep the best foals and show them."

"Have any suggestions?" she asked again, her voice breaking.

"Oh, yes. I know the perfect man for the job."

"I don't need a *perfect* man. I'm looking for someone a little unpredictable, someone who takes big risks and risks making mistakes—but admits them."

"Someone a bit like yourself."

"That's right."

"You need a husband, Agnes. In particular, me."

Her heart caught in her throat. Crying a little, she took his face between her hands. The teasing was over. "You're not going back to England? What about your career at Scotland Yard?"

"I've learned too much about myself to go back to that. Too much that I like. Pleasant surprises." He smoothed her tears away and said in a husky voice, "Are you crying because you're happy or because you didn't want me to propose marriage to you?"

Agnes stroked his hair. "Happy."

He put both arms around her waist and pulled her up with him as he got to his knees again. She tilted her head back and smiled at him in the moonlight. "Please keep me at the center of your heart forever," he said softly.

Aggie made a sound of devotion. She knew where he'd read those words, and how many centuries had passed since a man had spoken them to the woman he loved. And she knew what to say in return. "Not one day will pass without you there. Keep me close in your heart, as well. You'll never have to look any farther than that, to find me."

John cupped a hand along her face. "Marry me." His voice was a low croon of persuasion. "Marry me. I love you so much. We'll carry the family torch for another eight hundred years, at least. And we'll make the kind of life we've *both* dreamed about."

"Yes. Oh, yes."

She touched his smile. He drew her back to the sand and began undressing her. "Would you like to be improper, my lady?" he whispered against her lips.

Aggie felt as if she were floating on dreams. "Even worse than that." He laughed until she unbuttoned his shirt and began kissing the center of his chest. "Welcome to Camelot," she said softly.

His arms went around her. "It's so good to be home."

# THE EDITOR'S CORNER

*And what is so rare as a day in June?*
*Then, if ever, come perfect days . . .*

With apologies to James Russell Lowell I believe we can add *and perfect reading, too,* from LOVESWEPT and FANFARE . . .

As fresh and beautiful as the rose in its title SAN ANTONIO ROSE, LOVESWEPT #474, by Fran Baker is a thrilling way to start your romance reading next month. Rafe Martinez betrayed Jeannie Crane, but her desire still burned for the only man she'd ever loved, the only man who'd ever made love to her. Rafe was back and admitting to her that her own father had driven him away. When he learned her secret, Rafe had a sure-fire way to get revenge . . . but would he? And could Jeannie ever find a way to tame the maverick who still drove her wild with ecstasy? This unforgettable love story will leave you breathless. . . .

Perfect in its powerful emotion is TOUGH GUY, SAVVY LADY, LOVESWEPT #475, by Charlotte Hughes. Charlotte tells a marvelous story of overwhelming love and stunning self-discovery in this tale of beautiful Honey Buchannan and Lucas McKay. Lucas smothered her with his love, sweetly dominating her life—and when she leaves he is distraught, but determined to win her back. Lucas has always hidden his own fears—he's a man who has pulled himself up by his boot straps to gain fortune and position—but to recapture the woman who is his life, he is going to have to change. TOUGH GUY, SAVVY LADY will touch you deeply . . . and joyfully.

Little could be so rare as being trapped IN A GOLDEN WEB, Courtney Henke's LOVESWEPT #476. Heroine Elizabeth Hamner is desperate! Framed for a crime she didn't commit, she's driven to actions she never dreamed she was capable of taking. And kidnapping gorgeous hunk Dexter Wolffe and forcing him to take her to Phoenix is just the start. Dex plays along—finding the beautiful bank manager the most delectable adversary he's ever encountered. He wants to kiss her defiant mouth and make her his prisoner . . . of love. You'll thrill to the romance of these two loners on the lam in one of LOVESWEPT's most delightful offerings ever!

And a dozen American beauties to Glenna McReynolds for her fabulously inventive OUTLAW CARSON, LOVESWEPT #478. We'll wager you've never run into a hero like Kit Carson before. Heroine Kristine Richards certainly hasn't. When the elusive, legendary Kit shows up at her university, Kristine can only wonder if he's a smuggler, a scholar—or a blessing from heaven, sent to shatter her senses. Kit is shocked by Kristine . . . for he had never believed before meeting her that there was any woman on earth who could arouse in him such fierce hunger . . . or such desperate jealousy. Both are burdened with secrets and wary of each other and have a long and difficult labyrinth to struggle through. But there are glimpses ahead of a Shangri-la just for them! As dramatic and surprising as a budding rose in winter, OUTLAW CARSON will enchant you!

Welcome to Tonya Wood who makes her debut with us with a real charmer in LOVESWEPT #477, GORGEOUS. Sam Christie was just too good-looking to be real. And too talented. And women were always throwing themselves at him. Well, until Mercy Rose Sullivan appeared in his life. When Mercy rescued Sam from the elevator in their apartment building, he can't believe what an endearing gypsy she is—or that she doesn't recognize him! Mercy is as feisty as she is guileless and puts up a terrific fight against Sam's long, slow, deep kisses. His fame is driving them apart just as love is bursting into full bloom . . . and it seems that only a miracle can bring these two dreamers together, where they belong. Sheer magical romance!

What is more perfect to read about on a perfect day than a lone, lean, mean deputy sheriff and a lady locksmith who's been called to free him from the bed he is handcuffed to? Nothing! So run to pick-up your copy of SILVER BRACELETS, LOVESWEPT #479, by Sandra Chastain. You'll laugh and cry and root for these two unlikely lovers to get together. Sarah Wilson is as tenderhearted as they come. Asa Canyon is one rough, tough hombre who has always been determined to stay free of emotional entanglements. They taste ecstasy together . . . but is Sarah brave enough to risk loving such a man? And can Asa dare to believe that a woman will always be there for him? A romance as vivid and fresh and thrilling as a crimson rose!

And don't forget FANFARE next month with its irresistible longer fiction.

First, STORM WINDS by Iris Johansen. This thrilling, sweeping novel set against the turbulent times of the French Revolution continues with stories of those whose lives are touched by the fabled Wind Dancer. Two unforgettable pairs of lovers will have you singing the praises of Iris Johansen all summer long! DREAMS TO KEEP by Nomi Berger is a powerfully moving novel of a memorable and courageous woman, a survivor of the Warsaw ghetto, who defies all odds and builds a life and a fortune in America. But she is a woman who will risk everything for revenge on the man who condemned her family . . . until a love that is larger than life itself gives her a vision of a future of which she'd never dreamed. And all you LOVESWEPT readers will know you have to be sure to get a copy of MAGIC by Tami Hoag in which the fourth of the "fearsome foursome" gets a love for all time. This utterly enchanting love story shows off the best of Tami Hoag! Remember, FANFARE signals that something great is coming. . . .

Enjoy your perfect days to come with perfect reading from LOVESWEPT and FANFARE!

With every good wish,

*Carolyn Nichols*

Carolyn Nichols
Editor
LOVESWEPT
Bantam Books
666 Fifth Avenue
New York, NY 10103

A fiercely independant woman, a proud and stubborn man -- bound by passion, torn apart by injustice.

# THE BELOVED WOMAN
# by Deborah Smith

The Trail of Tears: The forced exodus of the Cherokee people from their homeland in Georgia to make way for the white gold miners and settlers. Katherine Blue Song's family never lived to see the Trail of Tears -- they were massacred just as she returned from Philadelphia, where she'd been one of the country's first women trained as a doctor.

Justis Gallatin, a white man, a rough and ready man, was Jesse Blue Song's friend and partner. Before he buried the victims of the massacre, he made a solemn promise to protect Katherine. But the lovely and head-strong Cherokee healer would not be protected or owned by any man -- her destiny was with her own people, to use her skills on the long arduous journey westward.

**The Beloved Woman** is a novel which traces the lives of two people caught up in the tide of history, who are hurtled together a passion as vast as the lands they loved, lost, and fought to regain.

On sale in March wherever Bantam Fanfare Books are sold.

AN209 -- 2/91